T0115951

PRAISE FOR **NUMERO ZERO**

"Witty and wry . . . slim in pages but plump in satire about modern Italy . . . It's hard not to be charmed by the zest of the author."

—*New York Times Book Review*

"Frequently imitated for his amalgamation of intellect, conspiracism, and historical suspense, the author of *The Name of the Rose* takes a more contemporary and satirical turn . . . Readers of Elena Ferrante or Rachel Kushner will likely catch the barbs in his clever absurdities."

—*Vulture*

"Although *Numero Zero* takes place in 1992, Eco may as well be describing our current journalistic landscape of hot takes and click bait. How do we process the overload? The implication is that we can't. Not only that, but the whole purpose is to overwhelm us, to keep us from understanding how everything adds up. If this sounds cynical, it is, although it's also compelling, a kind of contextual lament."

—*Los Angeles Times*

"A smart puzzle and a delight."

—*Kirkus Reviews*, starred review

"Eco combines his delight in suspense with astute political satire in this brainy, funny, neatly lacerating thriller . . . Eco's caustically clever, darkly hilarious, dagger-quick tale of lies, crimes, and collusions condemns the shameless corruption and greed undermining journalism and governments everywhere. A satisfyingly scathing indictment brightened by resolute love."

—*Booklist*

PRAISE FOR **UMBERTO ECO**

"One of the most influential thinkers of our time."

—*Los Angeles Times*

"Once the reader gets on the Eco carousel it's hard to get off."

—*New York Times*

"Eco is one of literature's greatest optimists." —*Telegraph*

"What his fiction and literary criticism have in common is a winning combination of tremendous erudition and delightful playfulness."

—*Jewish Chronicle*

"True wit and wisdom coexist with fierce scholarship inside Umberto Eco, a writer who actually knows a thing or two about being truly human."

—*Buffalo News*

"A sophisticated, agile mind."

—*Publishers Weekly*

"[Eco has] profound erudition, lively wit, and passion for ideas of all shapes and sizes . . . [His] pleasure in such explorations is obvious and contagious."

—*Booklist*

"Eco's medieval erudition gives him a magisterial perspective on contemporary culture."

—*Toronto Star*

"Eco combines scholarship with a love of paradox and a quirky, sometimes outrageous, sense of humor."

—*Atlantic*

ALSO BY UMBERTO ECO

The Prague Cemetery
The Mysterious Flame of Queen Loana
Baudolino
The Island of the Day Before
Foucault's Pendulum
The Name of the Rose
Inventing the Enemy

Confessions of a Young Novelist
The Infinity of Lists
On Ugliness
History of Beauty
Turning Back the Clock
On Literature
Five Moral Pieces
Kant and the Platypus
Serendipities
How to Travel with a Salmon
Six Walks in the Fictional Woods
Misreadings
Travels in Hyperreality
Semiotics and the Philosophy of Language
A Theory of Semiotics
The Open Work

UMBERTO ECO

NUMERO ZERO

Translated from the Italian by Richard Dixon

MARINER BOOKS
HOUGHTON MIFFLIN HARCOURT
BOSTON • NEW YORK

First Mariner Books edition 2016

First U.S. edition
Copyright © 2015 by Bompiani / RCS Libri S.p.A.
English translation copyright © 2015 by Richard Dixon
First published in Great Britain in 2015 by Harvill Secker

All rights reserved

For information about permission to reproduce selections from this book, write to trade.permissions@hmhco.com or to Permissions, Houghton Mifflin Harcourt Publishing Company, 3 Park Avenue, 19th Floor, New York, New York 10016.

www.hmhco.com

Library of Congress Cataloging-in-Publication Data is available.
ISBN 978-0-544-63508-1 (hardback) ISBN 978-0-544-81183-6 (pbk.)
ISBN 978-0-544-66826-3 (trade paper international edition)

Printed in the United States of America
DOC 10 9 8 7 6 5 4 3 2 1

This book was originally published in Italian with the title *Numero Zero* by Bompiani, Milan, 2015.

For Anita

Only connect!

— E. M. FORSTER

Contents

NUMERO ZERO

1

Saturday, June 6, 1992, 8 a.m.

No water in the tap this morning.

Gurgle, gurgle, two sounds like a baby's burp, then nothing.

I knocked next door: everything was fine there. You must have closed the valve, she said. Me? I don't even know where it is. Haven't been here long, you know, don't get home till late. Good heavens! But don't you turn off the water and gas when you're away for a week? Me, no. That's pretty careless. Let me come in, I'll show you.

She opened the cupboard beneath the sink, moved something, and the water was on. See? You'd turned it off. Sorry, I wasn't thinking. Ah, you *singles!* Exit neighbor: now even she talks English.

Keep calm. There are no such things as poltergeists, only in films. And I'm no sleepwalker, but even if I had sleepwalked, I wouldn't have known anything about the valve or I'd have closed it when I couldn't sleep, because the shower leaks and I'm always liable to spend the night wide-eyed listening to the dripping, like

Chopin at Valldemossa. In fact, I often wake up, get out of bed, and shut the bathroom door so I don't hear that goddamn drip.

It couldn't have been an electrical contact (it's a hand valve, it can only be worked by hand), or a mouse, which, even if there was a mouse, would hardly have had the strength to move such a contraption. It's an old-fashioned tap (everything in this apartment dates back at least fifty years) and rusty besides. So it needed a hand. Humanoid. And I don't have a chimney down which the Ourang-Outang of Rue Morgue could have climbed.

Let's think. Every effect has its cause, or so they say. We can rule out a miracle—I can't see why God would worry about my shower, it's hardly the Red Sea. So, a natural effect, a natural cause. Last night before going to bed, I took a sleeping pill with a glass of water. Obviously the water was still running then. This morning it wasn't. So, my dear Watson, the valve had been closed during the night—and not by you. Someone was in my house, and he, they, were afraid I might have been disturbed, not by the noise they were making (they were silent as the grave) but by the drip, which might have irritated even them, and perhaps they wondered why I didn't stir. And, very craftily, they did what my neighbor would have done: they turned off the water.

And then? My books are in their usual disarray, half the world's secret services could have gone through them page by page without my noticing. No point looking in the drawers and opening the cupboard in the corridor. If they wanted to make a discovery, there's only one thing to do these days: rummage through the computer. Perhaps they'd copied everything so as not to waste time and gone back home. And only now, opening and reopening each document, they'd have realized there was nothing in the computer that could possibly interest them.

What were they hoping to find? It's obvious—I mean, I can't see any other explanation—they were looking for something to do with the newspaper. They're not stupid, they'd have assumed I must have made notes about all the work we are doing in the newsroom—and therefore that, if I knew anything about the Braggadocio business, I'd have written it down somewhere. Now they'll have worked out the truth, that I keep everything on a diskette. Last night, of course, they'd also have been to the office and found no diskette of mine. So they'll be coming to the conclusion (but only now) that I keep it in my pocket. What idiots we are, they'll be saying, we should have checked his jacket. Idiots? Shits. If they were smart, they wouldn't have ended up doing such a scummy job.

Now they'll have another go, at least until they arrive at the stolen letter. They'll arrange for me to be jostled in the street by fake pickpockets. So I'd better get moving before they try again. I'll send the diskette to a poste restante address and decide later when to pick it up. What on earth am I thinking of, one man is already dead, and Simei has flown the nest. They don't even need to know if I know, and what I know. They'll get rid of me just to be on the safe side, and that's the end of it. I can hardly go around telling the newspapers I knew nothing about the whole business, since just by saying it I'd make it clear I knew what had happened.

How did I end up in this mess? I think it's all the fault of Professor Di Samis and the fact that I know German.

• • •

What makes me think of Di Samis, a business of decades ago? I've always blamed Di Samis for my failure to graduate, and it's all because I never graduated that I ended up in this mess. And then Anna left me after two years of marriage because she'd come to realize, in her words, that I was a compulsive loser—God knows what I must have told her at the time to make myself look good.

I never graduated due to the fact that I know German. My grandmother came from South Tyrol and made me speak it when I was young. Right from my first year at university I'd taken to translating books from German to pay for my studies. Just knowing German was a profession at the time. You could read and translate books that others didn't understand (books regarded as important then), and you were paid better than translators from French and even from English. Today I think the same is true of those who know Chinese or Russian. In any event, either you translate or you graduate; you can't do both. Translation means staying at home, in the warmth or the cold, working in your slippers and learning tons of things in the process. So why go to university lectures?

I decided on a whim to register for a German course. I wouldn't have to study much, I thought, since I already knew it all. The luminary at that time was Professor Di Samis, who had created what the students called his eagle's nest in a dilapidated Baroque palace where you climbed a grand staircase to reach a large atrium. On one side was Di Samis's establishment, on the other the *aula magna,* as the professor pompously called it, a lecture hall with fifty or so seats.

You could enter his establishment only if you put on felt slippers. At the entrance there were enough for the assistants and two or three students. Those without slippers had to wait their turn outside. Everything was polished to a high gloss, even, I think, the books on the walls. And even the faces of the elderly assistants who had been waiting their chance for a teaching position from time immemorial.

The lecture hall had a lofty vaulted ceiling and Gothic windows (I never understood why, in a Baroque palace) with green stained glass. At the correct time, which is to say at fourteen minutes past the hour, Professor Di Samis emerged from the institute, followed at a distance of one meter by his oldest assistant and at two meters by the younger ones, those under fifty. The oldest assistant carried his books, the younger ones the tape recorder—tape recorders at that time were still enormous, and looked like a Rolls-Royce.

Di Samis covered the ten meters that separated the institute from the hall as though they were twenty: he didn't follow a straight line but a curve (whether a parabola or an ellipse I'm not sure), proclaiming loudly, "Here we are, here we are!" Then he entered the lecture hall and sat down on a kind of carved podium, waiting to begin with Call me Ishmael.

The green light from the stained-glass windows gave a cadaverous appearance to the face that smiled malevolently, as the assistants set up the tape recorder. Then he began: "Contrary to what my valiant colleague Professor Bocardo has said recently . . ." and so on for two hours.

That green light sent me into a watery slumber, to be seen also in the eyes of his assistants. I shared their suffering. At the end of the two hours, while we students swarmed out, Professor Di Samis had the tape rewound, stepped down from the podium, seated himself democratically in the front row with his assistants, and together they all listened again to the two-hour lecture, while the professor nodded with satisfaction at each passage he considered essential. It should be noted that the course was on the translation of the Bible in the German of Luther. What a phenomenon, my classmates would say with a forlorn expression.

At the end of the second year, attending infrequently, I ventured to ask whether I could do my thesis on irony in Heine. (I found it consoling the way that he treated unhappy experiences of love with what I felt to be appropriate cynicism—I was preparing for my own experiences of love.) "You young people, you young people," Di Samis would say sadly, "you want to hurl yourselves immediately at modern authors."

I understood, in a sort of flash, that there was no hope of doing the thesis with Di Samis. Then I thought of Professor Ferio, who was younger and enjoyed a reputation for dazzling intelligence, and who studied the romantic period and around there. But my older classmates warned me that, in any event, I would have Di Samis as second supervisor for the thesis, and not to approach Professor Ferio directly because Di Samis would immediately find out and swear eternal enmity. I had to go by an indirect route, as though Ferio had asked me to do the thesis with him, and De Samis would then take it out on him and not me. Di Samis hated Ferio for the simple reason that he himself had appointed Ferio as professor. At university (then, though still, I understand, today), things are the opposite of the ways of the normal world: it isn't the sons who hate the fathers, but the fathers who hate the sons.

I thought I'd be able to approach Ferio casually during one of the monthly conferences that Di Samis organized in his *aula magna,* attended by many colleagues, since he always succeeded in inviting famous scholars.

Things evolved as follows: Right after the conference was the debate, monopolized by professors. Then everyone left, the speaker having been invited to eat at La Tartaruga, the best restaurant in the area, mid-nineteenth-century style, with waiters in tailcoats. To get from the eagle's nest to the restaurant, one had to walk down a large porticoed street, then across a historic piazza, turn the corner of an elaborate building, and finally cross a smaller piazza. The speaker made his way along the porticoes surrounded by the senior professors, followed one meter behind by the associates, two meters behind by the younger associates, and trailing at a reasonable distance behind them, the bolder students. Having reached the historic piazza the students walked off, at the corner of the elaborate building the assistants took their leave, the associates crossed the smaller piazza and said goodbye at the entrance to the restaurant, where only the guest and the senior professors entered.

So it was that Professor Ferio never came to hear of my existence. In the meantime I fell out of love with the place and stopped attending. I translated like an automaton, but you have to take whatever they give you, and I was rendering a three-volume work on the role of Friedrich List in the creation of the *Zollverein,* the German Customs Union, in *dolce stil novo*. So you can understand why I gave up translating from German, but by now it was getting late to return to university.

The trouble is, you don't get used to the idea: you still feel sure that someday or other you'll complete all the exams and do your thesis. And anyone who nurtures impossible hopes is already a loser. Once you come to realize it, you just give up.

At first I found work as a tutor to a German boy, too stupid to go to school, in the Engadin. Excellent climate, acceptably isolated, and I held out for a year as the money was good. Then one day the boy's mother pressed herself against me in a corridor, letting me understand that she was available. She had buck teeth and a hint of a mustache, and I politely indicated that I wasn't of the same mind. Three days later I was fired because the boy was making no progress.

After that I made a living as a hack journalist. I wanted to write for magazines, but the only interest came from a few local newspapers, so I did things like reviews of provincial shows and touring companies, earning a pittance. I had just enough time to review the warm-up act, peeping from the wings at the dancing girls dressed in their sailor suits and following them to the milk bar, where they would order a suppertime caffè latte, and if they weren't too hard up, a fried egg. I had my first sexual experiences then, with a singer, in exchange for an indulgent write-up for a newspaper in Saluzzo.

I had no place I could call home. I lived in various cities (I moved to Milan once I received the call from Simei), checking proofs for at least three publishing houses (university presses, never for the large publishers), and edited the entries for an encyclopedia (which meant checking the dates, titles of works, and so on). Losers, like autodidacts, always know much more than winners. If you want to win, you need to know just one thing and not to waste your time on anything else: the pleasures of erudition are reserved for losers. The more a person knows, the more things have gone wrong.

I spent several years reading manuscripts that publishers (sometimes important ones) passed on to me, as in a publishing house no one has any wish to read the manuscripts that just turn up. They used to pay me five thousand lire per manuscript. I'd spend the whole day stretched out in bed reading furiously, then write an opinion on two sheets of paper, employing the best of my sarcasm to destroy the unsuspecting author, while at the publishing house there was a sigh of relief and a letter promptly dispatched to the improvident wretch: So sorry to say no, etc. etc. Reading manuscripts that are never going to be published can become a vocation.

Meanwhile there was the business with Anna, which ended as it had to end. After that I was never able (or have steadfastly refused) to find any interest in a woman, since I was afraid of messing it up again. I sought out sex for therapeutic purposes, the occasional casual encounter where you don't need to worry about falling in love, one night and that's it, thank you, and the occasional relationship for payment, so as not to become obsessed by desire.

All this notwithstanding, I dreamed what all losers dream, about one day writing a book that would bring me fame and fortune. To learn how to become a great writer, I became what in the last century was called the *nègre* (or ghostwriter, as they say today, to be politically correct) for an author of detective stories who gave himself an American name to improve sales, like the actors in spaghetti westerns. But I enjoyed working in the shadows, hidden behind a double veil (the Other's and the Other's other name).

Writing detective stories for somebody else was easy, all you had to do was imitate the style of Chandler or, at worst, Mickey Spillane. But when I tried writing a book of my own, I realized that in describing someone or something, I'd always be making cultural allusions: I couldn't just say that so-and-so was walking along on a bright cloudless afternoon, but would end up saying he was walking "beneath a Canaletto sky." I know that this was what D'Annunzio used to do: in order to say that a certain Costanza Landbrook had a particular quality, he would write that she seemed like a creation of Thomas Lawrence; of Elena Muti he observed that her features recalled certain profiles of early Moreau, and that Andrea Sperelli reminded him of the portrait of the unknown gentleman in the Borghese Gallery. And to understand what's going on in a novel, you had to thumb through issues of art history magazines on sale in the bookstalls.

If D'Annunzio was a bad writer, that didn't mean I had to be one. To rid myself of the habit of citing others, I decided not to write at all.

In short, mine hadn't been much of a life. And now, at my age, I receive Simei's invitation. Why not? Might as well try it.

What do I do? If I stick my nose outside, I'll be taking a risk. It's better to wait here. There are some boxes of crackers and cans of meat in the kitchen. I still have half a bottle of whiskey left over from last night. It might help to pass a day or two. I'll pour a few drops (and then perhaps a few more, but only in the afternoon, since drinking in the morning numbs the mind) and try to go back to the beginning of this adventure, no need to refer to my diskette. I recall everything quite clearly, at least at the moment.

Fear of death concentrates the mind.

2

Monday, April 6, 1992

"A BOOK?" I ASKED SIMEI.

"A book. The memoirs of a journalist, the story of a year's work setting up a newspaper that will never be published. The title of the newspaper is to be *Domani,* tomorrow, which sounds like a slogan for our government: tomorrow, we'll talk about it tomorrow! So the title of the book has to be *Domani: Yesterday.* Good, eh?"

"And you want me to write the book? Why not write it yourself? You're a journalist, no? At least, given you're about to run a newspaper . . ."

"Running a newspaper doesn't necessarily mean you know how to write. The minister of defense doesn't necessarily know how to lob a hand grenade. Naturally, throughout the coming year we'll discuss the book day by day, you'll give it the style, the pep, I'll control the general outline."

"You mean we'll both appear as authors, or will it be Colonna interviewing Simei?"

"No, no, my dear Colonna, the book will appear under my name. You'll have to disappear after you've written it. No offense, but you'll be a *nègre.* Dumas had one, I don't see why I can't have one too."

"And why me?"

"You have some talent as a writer—"

"Thank you."

"—and no one has ever noticed it."

"Thanks again."

"I'm sorry, but up to now you've only worked on provincial newspapers, you've been a cultural slave for several publishing houses, you've written a novel for someone (don't ask me how, but I happened to pick it up, and it works, it has a certain style), and at the age of fifty or so you've raced here at the news that I might perhaps have a job for you. So you know how to write, you know what a book is, but you're still scraping around for a living. No need to be ashamed. I too—if I'm about to set up a newspaper that will never get published, it's because I've never been short-listed for the Pulitzer Prize. I've only ever run a sports weekly and a men's monthly—for men alone, or lonely men, whichever you prefer."

"I could have some self-respect and say no."

"You won't, because I'm offering you six million lire per month for a year, in cash, off the books."

"That's a lot for a failed writer. And then?"

"And then, when you've delivered the book, let's say around six months after the end of the experiment, another ten million lire, lump sum, in cash. That will come from my own pocket."

"And then?"

"And then that's your affair. You'll have earned more than eighty million lire, tax free, in eighteen months, if you don't spend it all on women, horses, and champagne. You'll be able to take it easy, look around."

"Let me get this straight. You're offering me six million lire a month—and (if I may say so) who knows how much you're getting out of this—there'll be other journalists to pay, to say nothing of the costs of production and printing and distribution, and you're telling me someone, a publisher I imagine, is ready to back this experiment for a year, then do nothing with it?"

"I didn't say he'll do nothing with it. He'll gain his own benefit from it. But me, no, not if the newspaper isn't published. Of course, the publisher might decide in the end that the newspaper must appear, but at that point it'll become big business and I doubt he'll want me around to look after it. So I'm ready for the publisher to decide at the end of this year that the experiment has produced the expected results and that he can shut up shop. That's why I'm covering myself: if all else fails, I'll publish the book. It'll be a bombshell and should give me a tidy sum in royalties. Alternatively, so to speak, there might be someone who won't want it published and who'll give me a sum of money, tax free."

"I follow. But maybe, if you want me to work as a loyal collaborator, you'll need to tell me who's paying, why the

Domani project exists, why it's perhaps going to fail, and what you're going to say in the book that, modesty aside, will have been written by me."

"All right. The one who's paying is Commendator Vimercate. You'll have heard of him . . ."

"Vimercate. Yes I have. He ends up in the papers from time to time: he controls a dozen or so hotels on the Adriatic coast, owns a large number of homes for pensioners and the infirm, has various shady dealings around which there's much speculation, and controls a number of local TV channels that start at eleven at night and broadcast nothing but auctions, telesales, and a few risqué shows . . ."

"And twenty or so publications."

"Rags, I recall, celebrity gossip, magazines such as *Them, Peeping Tom,* and weeklies about police investigations, like *Crime Illustrated, What They Never Tell Us,* all garbage, trash."

"Not all. There are also specialist magazines on gardening, travel, cars, yachting, *Home Doctor.* An empire. A nice office this, isn't it? There's even the ornamental fig, like you find in the offices of the kingpins in state television. And we have an *open plan,* as they say in America, for the news team, a small but dignified office for you, and a room for the archives. All rent-free, in this building that houses all the Commendatore's companies. For the rest, each dummy issue will use the same production and printing facilities as the other magazines, so the cost of the experiment is kept to an acceptable level. And we're practically in the city center, unlike the big newspapers where you have to take two trains and a bus to reach them."

"But what does the Commendatore expect from this experiment?"

"The Commendatore wants to enter the inner sanctum of finance, banking, and perhaps also the quality papers. His way of getting there is the promise of a new newspaper ready to tell the truth about everything. Twelve zero issues—0/1, 0/2, and so on—dummy issues printed in a tiny number of exclusive copies that the Commendatore will inspect, before arranging for them to be seen by certain people he knows. Once the Commendatore has shown he can create problems for the so-called inner sanctum of finance and politics, it's likely they'll ask him to put a stop to such an idea. He'll close down *Domani* and will then be given an entry permit to the inner sanctum. He buys up, let's say, just two percent of shares in a major newspaper, a bank, a major television network."

I let out a whistle. "Two percent is a hell of a lot! Does he have that kind of money?"

"Don't be naïve. We're talking about finance, not business. First buy, then wait and see where the money to pay for it comes from."

"I get it. And I can also see that the experiment would work only if the Commendatore keeps quiet about the newspaper not being published in the end. Everyone would have to think that the wheels of his press were eager to roll, so to speak."

"Of course. The Commendatore hasn't even told me about the newspaper not appearing. I suspect, or rather, I'm sure of it. And the colleagues we will meet tomorrow mustn't know. They have to work away, believing they are building their future. This is something only you and I know."

"But what's in it for you if you then write down all you've been doing to help along the Commendatore's blackmail?"

"Don't use the word 'blackmail.' We publish news. As the *New York Times* says, 'All the news that's fit to print.'"

"And maybe a little more."

"I see we understand each other. If the Commendatore then uses our dummy issues to intimidate someone, or wipes his butt with them, that's his business, not ours. But the point is, my book doesn't have to tell the story of what decisions were made in our editorial meetings. I wouldn't need you for that—a tape recorder would do. The book has to give the idea of another kind of newspaper, has to show how I labored away for a year to create a model of journalism independent of all pressure, implying that the venture failed because it was impossible to have a free voice. To do this, I need you to invent, idealize, write an epic, if you get my meaning."

"The book will say the opposite of what actually happened. Fine. But you'll be proved wrong."

"By whom? By the Commendatore, who would have to say no, the aim of the project was simple extortion? He'd be happier to let people think he'd been forced to quit because he too was under pressure, that he preferred to kill the newspaper so it didn't become a voice controlled by someone else. And our news team? Are they going to say we're wrong when the book presents them as journalists of the highest integrity?

It'll be a *betzeller* that nobody will be able or willing to attack."

"All right, seeing that both of us are men without qualities—if you'll excuse the allusion—I accept the terms."

"I like dealing with people who are loyal and say what they think."

3

Tuesday, April 7

First meeting with the editorial staff. Six, that should do.

Simei had told me I wouldn't have to traipse around doing bogus investigations, but was to stay in the office and keep a record of what was going on. And to justify my presence, this is how he started: "So gentlemen, let's get to know each other. This is Dottor Colonna, a man of great journalistic experience. He will work beside me, and for this reason we'll call him assistant editor; his main task will be checking all of your articles. Each of you comes from a different background, and it's one thing to have worked on a far-left paper and quite another to have experience of, let's say, the *Voice of the Gutter*, and since, as you see, we are a spartan few, those who have always worked on death notices may also have to write an editorial on the government crisis. It's therefore a question of uniformity of style and, if anyone is tempted to write 'palingenesis,' then Colonna will tell you not to, and will suggest an alternative word."

"Deep moral renewal," I said.

"There. And if anyone is tempted to describe a dramatic situation by saying we're in the 'eye of the storm,' I imagine Dottor Colonna will be just as quick to remind you that according to all scientific manuals, the 'eye of the storm' is the place where calm reigns while the storm rages all around."

"No, Dottor Simei," I interrupted. "In such a case I'd say you should use 'eye of the storm' because it doesn't matter what science says, readers don't know, and 'eye of the storm' gives exactly the idea of finding yourself in the middle of it. This is what the press and television have taught them."

"Excellent idea, Dottor Colonna. We have to talk on the same level as the reader, we don't want the sophisticated language of eggheads. Our proprietor once said that his television audience had an average mental age of twelve. That's not the case with us, but it's always useful to put an age on your readers. Ours ought to be over fifty, they'll be good, honest, middle-class folk, eager for law and order but desperate to read gossip and revelations about other people's misfortunes. We'll start off from the principle that they're not what you'd call great readers, in fact most of them won't have a book in the house, though, when they have to, they'll talk about the latest book that's selling millions of copies around the world. Our readers may not read books, but they are fascinated by great eccentric painters who sell for billions. Likewise, they'll never get to see the film star with long legs and yet they want to know all about her secret love life. Now let's allow the others to introduce themselves. We'll start with the only female . . . Signorina, or Signora . . ."

"Maia Fresia. Unmarried, single, or spinster, take your choice. Twenty-eight. I nearly graduated in literature but had to stop for family reasons. I worked for five years on a gossip magazine. My job was to go around the entertainment world and sniff out who was having an affair with whom and to get photographers to lie in wait for them. More often I had to persuade a singer or actress to invent a flirtation with another celebrity, and I'd take them to the appointment with the paparazzi, the two walking hand in hand, or taking a furtive kiss. I enjoyed it at first, but now I'm tired of writing such drivel."

"And why, my dear, did you agree to join our venture?"

"I imagine a daily newspaper will be covering more serious matters, and I'll have a chance to make a name for investigations that have nothing to do with celebrity romance. I'm curious, and think I'll be a good sleuth."

She was slim and spoke with cautious gaiety.

"Excellent. And you?"

"Romano Braggadocio."

"Strange name, where's it from?"

"Ha, that's one of the many crosses I have to bear in life. Apparently it has a pretty unattractive meaning in English, though not in other languages. My grandfather was a foundling, and you know how surnames in such cases used to be invented by a public official. If he was a sadist, he could even call you Ficarotta, but in my grandfather's case the official was only moderately sadistic and had a certain learning. As for me,

I specialize in digging for dirt, and I used to work for *What They Don't Tell Us,* one of our own publisher's magazines. I was never taken on full-time, they paid me per article."

As for the other four, Cambria had spent his nights in casualty wards and police stations gathering the latest news—an arrest, a death in a high-speed pileup on the highway—and had never succeeded in getting any further; Lucidi inspired mistrust at first glance and had worked on publications that no one had ever heard of; Palatino came from a long career in weekly magazines of games and assorted puzzles; Costanza had worked as a subeditor, correcting proofs, but newspapers nowadays had too many pages, no one could proof everything before it went to press, and even the major newspapers were now writing "Simone de Beauvoire," or "Beaudelaire," or "Roosvelt," and the proofreader was becoming as outmoded as the Gutenberg press. None of these fellow travelers came from particularly inspiring backgrounds—a *Bridge of San Luis Rey*—and I have no idea how Simei had managed to track them down.

Once the introductions were over, Simei outlined the different aspects of the newspaper.

"So then, we'll be setting up a daily newspaper. Why *Domani*? Because traditional papers gave (and still give) the previous evening's news, and that's why they called them *Corriere della Sera, Evening Standard,* or *Le Soir.* These days we've already seen yesterday's news on the eight o'clock television news the previous evening, so the newspapers are always telling you what you already know, and that's why sales keep falling. *Domani* will summarize the news that now stinks like rotten fish, but it will do so in one small column that can be read in a few minutes."

"So what will the paper cover?" asked Cambria.

"A daily newspaper is destined to become more like a weekly magazine. We'll be talking about what might happen tomorrow, with feature articles, investigative supplements, unexpected predictions . . . I'll give you an example. There's a bomb blast at four in the afternoon. By the next day everyone knows about it. Well, from four until midnight, before going to press, we have to dig up someone who can provide something entirely new about the likely culprits, something the police don't yet know, and to sketch out a scenario of what will happen over the coming weeks as a result of the attack."

Braggadocio: "But to launch an investigation of that kind in eight hours, you'd need an editorial staff at least ten times our size, along with a wealth of contacts, informers, or whatever."

"That's right, and when the newspaper is actually up and running, that's how it will have to be. But for now, over the next year, we only have to show it can be done. And it *can* be done, because each dummy issue can carry whatever date we fancy, and it can perfectly well demonstrate how the newspaper would have treated it months earlier when, let's say, the bomb had gone off. In that case, we already know what will fall, but we'll be talking as though the reader doesn't yet know. So all our news leaks will take on the flavor of something fresh, surprising, dare I say oracular. In other words, we have to say to our owner: this is how *Domani* would have been had it appeared yesterday. Understood? And, if we wanted to, even if no one had actually thrown the bomb, we could easily do an issue *as if.*"

"Or throw the bomb ourselves if we felt like it," sneered Braggadocio.

"Let's not be silly," cautioned Simei. Then, almost as an afterthought, "And if you really want to do that, don't come telling me."

After the meeting I found myself walking with Braggadocio. "Haven't we already met?" he asked. I thought we hadn't, and he said perhaps I was right, but with a slightly suspicious air, and he instantly adopted a familiar tone. Simei had established a certain formality with the editorial staff, and I myself tend to keep a distance from people, unless we've been to bed together, but Braggadocio was eager to stress that we were colleagues. I didn't want to seem like someone who puts on airs just because Simei had introduced me as editor in chief or whatever it was. In any event, I was curious about him and had nothing better to do.

He took me by the arm and suggested we go for a drink at a place he knew. He smiled with his fleshy lips and slightly bovine eyes, in a way that struck me as vaguely obscene. Bald as von Stroheim, his nape vertical to his neck, but his face was that of Telly Savalas, Lieutenant Kojak. There—always some allusion.

"Cute little thing, that Maia, no?"

I was embarrassed to admit that I'd hardly looked at her. I told him I kept my distance from women. He shook my arm: "Don't play the gentleman, Colonna. I saw you watching her on the sly. I think she'd be up for it. The truth is, all women are up for it, you just have to know which way to take them. A bit too thin for my taste, flat boobs, but all in all, she'd do."

We arrived at Via Torino and made a sharp turn at a church, into a badly lit alley. Many doors there had been shut tight for God knows how long, and no shops, as if the place had long been abandoned. A rancid smell seemed to hang over it, but this must just have been synesthesia, from the peeling walls covered in fading graffiti. High up was a pipe that let out smoke, and you couldn't work out where it came from, since the upper windows were bricked up as though no one lived there anymore. Perhaps it was a pipe that came from a house that opened on another side, and no one was worried about smoking out an abandoned alley.

"This is Via Bagnera, Milan's narrowest street, though not as narrow as Rue du Chat-qui-Pêche in Paris, where you can't walk along side by side. They call it Via Bagnera but once it was called Stretta Bagnera, and before that Stretta Bagnaria, named after some public baths that were here in Roman times."

At that moment a woman appeared around a corner with a stroller. "Either reckless or badly informed," commented Braggadocio. "If I were a woman, I wouldn't be walking along here, especially in the dark. They could knife you as soon as look at you. What a shame that would be, such a waste of a pert little creature like her, a good little mother happy to get fucked by the plumber. Look, turn around, see how she wiggles her hips. Murderous deeds have taken place here. Behind these doors, now bricked up, there must still be abandoned cellars and perhaps secret passages. Here, in the nineteenth century, a certain artless wretch called Antonio Boggia enticed a bookkeeper into downstairs rooms to check over some accounts and attacked him with a hatchet. The victim managed to escape, and Boggia was arrested, judged insane, and locked up in a lunatic asylum for two years. As soon as he was released he was back to hunting out rich and gullible folk, luring them into his cellar, robbing them, murdering them, and burying them there. A serial killer, as we'd say today, but an imprudent one, since he left evidence of his commercial transactions with the victims and in the end was caught. The police dug down in the cellar, found five or six bodies, and Boggia was hanged near Porta Ludovica. His head was given to the anatomical laboratory at the Ospedale Maggiore—it was the days of Cesare Lombroso, when they were looking at the cranium and facial features for signs of congenital criminality. Then it seems the head was buried in the main cemetery, but who knows, relics of that kind were tasty morsels for occultists and maniacs of all kinds . . . Here you can feel the presence of Boggia, even today, like being in the London of Jack the Ripper. I wouldn't want to spend the night here, yet it intrigues me. I come back often, arrange meetings here."

From Via Bagnera we found ourselves in Piazza Mentana, and Braggadocio then took me into Via Morigi, another dark street, though with several small shops and decorative entrances. We reached an open space with a vast parking area surrounded by ruins. "You see," said Braggadocio, "those on the left are Roman ruins—almost no one remembers that Milan was once the capital of the empire. So they can't be touched, though there isn't the slightest interest in them. But those ruins behind the parking lot are what remains of houses bombed in the last war."

The bombed-out houses didn't have the timeworn tranquility of those ancient remains that now seemed reconciled with death, but peeped out sinisterly from their grim voids as though affected by lupus.

"I don't know why there's been no attempt to build in this area," said Braggadocio. "Perhaps it's protected, perhaps the owners make more money from the parking lot than from rental houses. But why leave evidence of the bombings? This area frightens me more than Via Bagnera, though it's good because it tells me what Milan was like after the war. Not many places bring back what the city was like almost fifty years ago. And this is the Milan I try to seek out, the place where I used to live as a child. The war ended when I was nine. Every now and then, at night, I still seem to hear the sound of bombing. But not just the ruins are left: look at the corner of Via Morigi, that tower dates back to the 1600s, and not even the bombs could bring it down. And below, come, there's this tavern, Taverna Moriggi, that dates back to the early 1900s—don't ask why the tavern has one *g* more than the road, the city authority must have gotten its street signs wrong, the tavern is much older, and that should be the correct spelling.

We walked into a large room with red walls and a bare ceiling from which hung an old wrought-iron chandelier, a stag's head at the bar, hundreds of dusty wine bottles along the walls, and bare wooden tables (it was before dinnertime, said Braggadocio, and they still had no tablecloths . . . later they'd put on those red-checked cloths and, to order, you had to study the writing on the blackboard, as in a French brasserie). At the tables were students, old-fashioned bohemian types with long hair—not in the '60s style but that of poets who once wore broad-brimmed hats and *lavallière* cravats—and a few old men in fairly high spirits; it was difficult to tell whether they had been there since the beginning of the century or whether the new proprietors had hired them as extras. We picked at a plate of cheeses, cured meats, and *lardo di Colonnata,* and drank some extremely good merlot.

"Nice, eh?" said Braggadocio. "Seems like another world."

"But what attracts you to this Milan, which ought to have vanished?"

"I've told you, I like to see what I've almost forgotten, the Milan of my grandfather and of my father."

He had started to drink, his eyes began to shine, with a paper napkin he dried a circle of wine that had formed on the old wooden table.

"I have a pretty wretched family history. My grandfather was a Fascist leader in what was later called the ominous regime. And back in 1945, on April 25, he was spotted by a partisan as he was trying to slip away not far from here, in Via Cappuccio; they took him and shot him, right there at that corner. It wasn't until much later that my father found out. He, true to my grandfather's beliefs, had enlisted in 1943 with the Decima Mas commando unit, and had then been captured at Salò and sent off for a year to Coltano concentration camp. He got through it by the skin of his teeth, they couldn't find any real accusations against him, and then, in

1946, Togliatti gave the go-ahead for a general amnesty—one of those contradictions of history, the Fascists rehabilitated by the Communists, though perhaps Togliatti was right, we had to return to normality at all costs. But the normality was that my father, with his past, and the shadow of his father, was jobless, and supported by my seamstress mother. And he gradually let himself go, he drank, and all I remember about him is his face full of little red veins and watery eyes, as he rambled on about his obsessions. He didn't try to justify fascism (he no longer had any ideals), but said that to condemn fascism, the antifascists had told many hideous stories. He didn't believe in the six million Jews gassed in the camps. I mean, he wasn't one of those who, even today, argue there was no Holocaust, but he didn't trust the story that had been put together by the liberators. 'All exaggerated accounts,' he used to say. 'Some survivors say, or that's what I've read at least, that at the center of one camp the mountains of clothes belonging to the murdered were over a hundred meters high. A hundred meters? But do you realize,' he'd say, 'that a pile a hundred meters high, seeing it has to rise up like a pyramid, needs to have a base wider than the area of the camp?'"

"But didn't he realize that anyone who has a terrible experience tends to exaggerate when describing it? You witness a road accident and you describe how the bodies lay in a lake of blood. You're not trying to make them believe it was as large as Lake Como, you're simply trying to give the idea that there was a lot of blood. Put yourself in the position of someone remembering one of the most tragic experiences of his life—"

"I'm not denying it, but my father taught me never to take

news as gospel truth. The newspapers lie, historians lie, now the television lies. Did you see those news stories a year ago, during the Gulf War, about the dying cormorant covered in tar in the Persian Gulf? Then it was shown to be impossible for cormorants to be in the Gulf at that time of year, and the pictures had been taken eight years earlier, during the time of the Iran-Iraq War. Or, according to others, cormorants had been taken from the zoo and covered with crude oil, which was what they must have done with Fascist crimes. Let's be clear, I have no sympathy for the beliefs of my father and my grandfather, nor do I want to pretend that Jews were not murdered. But I no longer trust anything. Did the Americans really go to the Moon? It's not impossible that they staged the whole thing in a studio—if you look at the shadows of the astronauts after the Moon landing, they're not believable. And did the Gulf War really happen, or did they just show us old clips from the archives? There are lies all around us, and if you know they're feeding you lies, you've got to be suspicious all the time. I'm suspicious, I'm always suspicious. The only real proven thing, for me, is this Milan of many decades ago. The bombing actually happened, and what's more, it was done by the English, or the Americans."

"And your father?"

"He died an alcoholic when I was thirteen. And to rid myself of those memories, once I'd grown up, I decided to throw myself in the opposite direction. In 1968 I was already thirty, but I let my hair grow, wore a parka and a sweater, and joined a Maoist commune. Later I discovered not only that Mao had killed more people than Stalin and Hitler put together, but also that the Maoists may well have been infiltrated by the secret services. And so I stuck to being a journalist and hunting out conspiracies. That way, I managed to avoid getting caught up with the Red terrorists (and I had some dangerous friends). I'd lost all faith in everything, except for the certainty that there's always someone behind our backs waiting to deceive us."

"And now?"

"And now, if this newspaper takes off, maybe I've found a place where my discovery will be appreciated . . . I'm working on a story that . . . Apart from the newspaper, there might even be a book in it. And then . . . But let's change the subject, let's say we'll talk about it once I've put all the facts together . . . It's just that I have to get it done soon, I need the money. The few lire we're getting from Simei will go some way, but not enough."

"To live on?"

"No, to buy me a car. Obviously I'll have to get a loan, but I still have to pay. And I need it now, for my investigation."

"Sorry, you say you want to make money from your investigation to buy the car, but you need the car to do your investigation."

"To piece a number of things together I need to travel, visit a few places, perhaps interview some people. Without the car and having to go to the office each day, I have to put it together from memory, do it all in my head. As if that was the only problem."

"So what's the real problem?"

"Well, it's not that I'm indecisive, but to understand what

I have to do, I must put together all the data. A bit of data on its own means nothing, all of it together lets you understand what you were unable to see at first. You have to uncover what they're trying to hide from you."

"You're talking about your investigation?"

"No, I'm talking about choosing the car . . ."

He was drawing on the table with a finger dipped in wine, almost as if he were marking out a series of dots that had to be joined together to create a figure, like in a puzzle magazine.

"A car needs to be fast and classy, I'm certainly not looking for a minivan, and then for me it's either front-wheel drive or nothing. I was thinking of a Lancia Thema turbo sixteen-valve, it's one of the more expensive, almost sixty million lire. I could even attempt two hundred and thirty-five kilometers an hour and acceleration from a standstill in seven point two. That's almost the top."

"It's expensive."

"Not just that, but you have to go and search out the information they're hiding from you. Car ads, when they're not lying, are keeping quiet about something. You have to go through the specifications in the trade magazines, and you find it's one hundred and eighty-three centimeters wide."

"That's not good?"

"You don't even notice that in all the ads they give you the length, which certainly counts when it comes to parking or prestige, but they rarely give the width, which is pretty important if you have a small garage or a parking space that's even narrower, not to mention how many times you have to go around before you find a space wide enough for you to park.

Width is fundamental. You've got to aim somewhere under a hundred and seventy centimeters."

"You can find them, I suppose."

"Sure, but you're cramped in a car that's a hundred and seventy centimeters if there's someone next to you and you don't have enough space for your right elbow. And then you don't have all those conveniences of the wider cars that have a whole range of controls available for the right hand, just by the gears."

"And so?"

"You've got to make sure the instrument panel is fairly generous and there are controls on the steering wheel, so you don't have to fumble around with your right hand. And that's how I came up with the Saab Nine Hundred turbo, one hundred and sixty-eight centimeters, maximum speed two hundred and thirty, and we're down to fifty million."

"That's your car."

"Yes, but only in one little corner do they tell you it has an acceleration to eight-fifty, whereas ideally it should be at least seven, like in the Rover Two Twenty turbo, forty million, width a hundred and sixty-eight, maximum speed two hundred and thirty-five, and acceleration at six point six, a thunderbolt."

"And so that's where you ought to be going . . ."

"No, because it's only at the bottom of the specifications they tell you it has a height of a hundred and thirty-seven centimeters. Too low for a well-built individual like me, almost like a racer for young sporty types, whereas the Lancia is a hundred and forty-three high and the Saab a hundred and forty-four and you fit in there like a lord. And that's fine—if you're one of those sporty types, you don't go looking at the specifications, which are like the side effects of drugs, written so small on the information slips you don't notice that if you take them, you're going to die the next day. The Rover Two Twenty-five weighs only one thousand one hundred and eighty-five kilos—that's not much, if you run into a truck, it will rip you apart like nothing, whereas you need to look toward heavier cars with steel strengthening. I don't say a Volvo, which is built like a tank only too slow, but at least a Rover Eight Twenty TI, around fifty million, two hundred and thirty an hour, and one thousand four hundred and twenty kilos."

"But I imagine you ruled it out because . . ." I commented, now as paranoid as him.

"Because it has an acceleration of eight point two, it's a tortoise, it has no sprint. Like the Mercedes Two Eighty C, which might be a hundred and seventy-two wide but, apart from costing seventy-seven million, it has an acceleration of eight point eight. And then they tell you it's five months' delivery. Something else to bear in mind if you reckon that some of those I've mentioned say it's two months' wait, and others are ready right away. And why ready right away? Because no one wants them. Always beware. It seems as though right away they'll give you the Calibra turbo sixteen-valve, two hundred and forty-five kilometers an hour, full traction, acceleration six point eight, one hundred and sixty-nine wide, and little more than fifty million."

"Excellent, I'd say."

"No, because it weighs only one thousand one hundred and thirty-five, too light, and only one hundred and thirty-two high, worse than all the others, for a customer with loads of money but who's a dwarf. As if these were the only problems. What about luggage space? The roomiest is the Thema sixteen-valve turbo, but it's a hundred and seventy-five wide. Among the narrower ones, I looked at the Dedra Two Point Zero XL, with plenty of luggage space, but not only does it have an acceleration of nine point four, it weighs little more than one thousand two hundred kilos and does only two hundred and ten an hour."

"And so?"

"And so I don't know which way to turn. I'm busy thinking about the investigation, but I wake up at night comparing cars."

"And you know everything by heart?"

"I've drawn up charts. The trouble is, I've memorized them, but it becomes unbearable. I think cars have been designed so I can't buy them."

"Isn't that going a bit far?"

"Suspicions never go too far. Suspect, always suspect, that's the only way you get to the truth. Isn't that what science says?"

"That's what it says, and that's what it does."

"Bullshit, even science lies. Look at the story of cold fusion. They lied to us for months and then it was found to be total nonsense."

"But it was discovered."

"By who? The Pentagon, who may have wanted to cover

up an embarrassing incident. Perhaps the cold-fusion people were right and those who lied were the ones who say the others have lied."

"And that's fine for the Pentagon and the CIA, but you're not trying to tell me that all car magazines are in the hands of the secret services of the demoplutojudeocracy who are out to get you." I was trying to bring back a note of common sense.

"Oh yes?" he said with a bitter smile. "Those people have links to big American industry, to the Seven Sisters of petroleum. They are the ones who assassinated Enrico Mattei, something I really couldn't care less about, except that they're the very same people who had my grandfather shot by funding the partisans. You see how it's all linked together?"

The waiters were now putting on the tablecloths and giving us to understand that the moment had passed for anyone drinking just two glasses.

"There was a time when with two glasses you could stay till two in the morning," sighed Braggadocio, "but now even here they're only interested in customers with money. Perhaps one day they'll turn the place into a discotheque with strobe lights. Here it's all still real—don't get me wrong—but it's already reeking as if fake. Would you believe it, this place in the heart of Milan has been run for the past few years by Tuscans, so I'm told. I've nothing against Tuscans, they're probably quite decent people, but I always remember, when I was a child, someone mentioned the daughter of friends who had made a bad marriage, and one of our cousins exclaimed, 'They ought to put a wall up from coast to coast just below

Florence.' 'Below Florence?' my mother retorted. 'Farther north! Farther north!'"

As we were waiting for the bill, Braggadocio asked, almost in a whisper, "You couldn't do me a loan? I'll pay you back in two months."

"Me? But I'm broke, like you."

"Really? I've no idea what Simei pays you and I've no right to know. Anyway, no harm asking. But you'll pay the bill?"

That's how I got to know Braggadocio.

4

Wednesday, April 8

NEXT DAY WE HAD OUR first real editorial meeting. "Let's start," said Simei. "Let's start with the newspaper for February 18 of this year."

"Why February 18?" asked Cambria, who would distinguish himself from then on as always asking the most ridiculous questions.

"Because this winter, on February 17, the police raided the office of Mario Chiesa, president of the Pio Albergo Trivulzio and a leading figure in Milan's Socialist Party. I'm sure you all recall this: Chiesa had asked for bribes on a contract given to a cleaning company from Monza, a deal worth a hundred and forty million lire, on which he was demanding ten percent. You see how even an old people's home makes a pretty fine cow to milk. And it could hardly have been the first time; the cleaning company was tired of coughing up and reported Chiesa to the police. So the person who went to deliver the first installment of the agreed fourteen million arrived with a hidden camera and a microphone. The moment Chiesa had taken the money, the police burst into his office. In terror, he went to the drawer, grabbed another, larger bundle he'd already collected from someone else, and rushed to the bathroom to flush the banknotes down the toilet, but it was no use, he was in handcuffs before he could get rid of the cash. This is the story, as you all remember. So now, Cambria, you know what we have to report in our newspaper for the day after. Go to the archive, read up on the news for that day, and give us an opening column. Or rather, no—write us a nice little article, since, as I recall, there was no mention of this story on the television news that evening."

"Okay, boss. I'm off."

"Hold on, because this is where *Domani*'s entire mission comes into play. You'll remember that over the next few days they tried to play down the importance of the event. Bettino Craxi would say that Chiesa was just a small-time crook, and he was about to expel him from the Socialist Party, but what the reader couldn't have known on February 18 was that the prosecutors were still investigating, and that a new magistrate was emerging, a man called Antonio Di Pietro, a real mastiff—he's well known now, but at the time no one had ever heard of him. Di Pietro put the thumbscrews on Chiesa, discovered the Swiss bank accounts, made him confess that it wasn't an isolated case, and now he's slowly bringing to light a whole web of political corruption involving all parties. And the first effects have been felt these past few days—you've seen that the Christian Democrats and the Socialist Party have lost a hell of a lot of votes in the elections, and that the Northern League has come out stronger, riding the scandal with its scorn for the rulers in Rome. Arrests are coming thick and fast, the political parties are slowly collapsing, and there are those who say that now the Berlin Wall is down and the Soviet Union in pieces, the Americans no longer need to worry about manipulating political parties and have left everything in the hands of the magistrates —or perhaps, we might guess, the magistrates are following a script written by the American secret services . . . But let's not jump to conclusions for the moment. This is the situation today. No one on February 18 could have imagined what would happen. But *Domani* will imagine it and make a series of forecasts. And I'll give this article of suppositions and innuendoes to you, Lucidi, you are so skilled in the use of 'perhaps' and 'maybe' and will report what actually happened. Name a few politicians from among the various parties, implicate the Left as well, let it be understood that the newspaper is collecting other evidence, and say it in such a way as to put the fear of God into those who will be reading our issue number 0/1 knowing full well what has transpired since February. But they're going to ask themselves what there might be in a zero issue of today's date . . . Understood? So, to work."

"Why are you giving me the job?" asked Lucidi.

Simei gave him a strange look, as though he ought to have understood something that we hadn't: "Because I know you're pretty good at finding out what's being said and fitting it to those responsible."

• • •

Later, when the two of us were alone, I asked Simei what he had meant. "Don't breathe a word to anyone," he said, "but I believe Lucidi is tied up with the secret services and using journalism as a cover."

"You're saying he's a spy? Why would we want a spy on our staff?"

"Because it's of no consequence that he's spying on us. What can he say, other than what the secret services would find out by reading any of our dummy issues? But he could bring us information he's picked up while spying on others."

Simei may not be a great journalist, I thought, but he's a genius of his kind. And it reminded me of the comment attributed to an orchestral conductor, a great foul mouth, who described a musician by saying, "'E's a god of 'is kind—'e's the kind that's shit."

5

Friday, April 10

WHILE WE WERE STILL THINKING about what to put into issue number 0/1, Simei gave everyone a broad outline of the essential aspects of our work.

"So, Colonna, please demonstrate to our friends how it's possible to respect, or appear to respect, one fundamental principle of democratic journalism, which is separating fact from opinion. A great many opinions will be expressed in *Domani,* and they'll be clearly identified as such, but how do we show that elsewhere articles give only facts?"

"Simple," I said. "Take the major British or American newspapers. If they report, say, a fire or a car accident, then obviously they can't indulge in saying what they think. And so they introduce into the piece, in quotation marks, the statements of a witness, a man in the street, someone who represents public opinion. Those statements, once put in quotes, become facts—in other words, it's a fact that that person expressed that opinion. But it might be assumed that the journalist has only quoted someone who thinks like him. So there will be two conflicting statements to show, as a fact, that there are varying opinions on a particular issue, and the newspaper is taking account of this irrefutable fact. The trick lies in quoting first a trivial opinion and then another opinion that is more respectable, and more closely reflects the journalist's view. In this way, readers are under the impression that they are being informed about two facts, but they're persuaded to accept just one view as being more convincing. Let's give an example: a bridge has collapsed, a truck has fallen over the edge, and the driver has been killed. The article, after carefully reporting the facts, will say: We interviewed Signor Rossi, age forty-two, proprietor of a newsstand on the street corner. 'What do you expect? That's fate,' he says. 'I'm sorry for the poor driver, but it's the way things go.' Immediately after, there's Signor Bianchi, age thirty-four, a builder working on a nearby construction site, who'll say, 'The local authority's to blame, this bridge has had problems, they've known about it for some time.' Who is the reader going to identify with? With the one who's being critical, who's pointing the finger of blame. Clear? The problem is what to put in quotes, and how to do it. Let's try a couple of exercises. We'll start with you, Costanza. A bomb has exploded in Piazza Fontana."

Costanza thought for a moment, then unleashed: "Signor Rossi, age forty-one, local authority employee, who might have been in the bank when the bomb exploded, told us, 'I was not far away and felt the blast. It was horrendous. Someone is behind this with an agenda of their own, but we'll never find out who.' Signor Bianchi, age fifty, a barber, was also passing by at the time of the explosion, which he recalls as deafening and terrible, and commented, 'It has all the makings of an anarchist attack, there's no doubt about it.'"

"Excellent. Signorina Fresia, news arrives of the death of Napoleon."

"Well, I'd say that Monsieur Blanche (let's take his age and profession as read) tells us that perhaps it was unfair to imprison someone on that island whose life was already over—poor man, he too had a family. Monsieur Manzoni, or rather Manzonì, tells us, 'We have lost someone who has changed the world, from the Manzanares to the Rhine. A great man.'"

"Manzanares, that's good," Simei said, smiling. "But there are other ways of passing on opinions undetected. To know what to include in a newspaper, you have, as journalists say, to set the agenda. There's no end of news in this world. But why report an accident up here in the North, in Bergamo, and ignore another that's taken place down south in Messina? It's not the news that makes the newspaper, but the newspaper that makes the news. And if you know how to put four different news items together, then you can offer the reader a fifth. Here's a newspaper from the day before yesterday. On the same page: Milan, newborn child tossed into toilet; Pescara, brother not to blame for Davide's death; Amalfi, psychologist caring for anorexic daughter accused of fraud; Buscate, boy who killed an eight-year-old when he was fifteen released after fourteen years in reformatory. These four articles all appear on the same page, and the headline is 'Child Violence and Society.' They all certainly relate to acts of violence involving a child, but they are very different cases. Only one (the infanticide) involves violence by parents on a child; the business of the psychologist doesn't seem to relate to children, since the age of this anorexic girl isn't given; the story of the boy from Pescara proves, if anything, that no violence occurred and the boy died accidentally; and finally the Buscate case, on closer reading, involves a hoodlum of almost thirty, and the real news was fourteen years ago. So what is the newspaper saying on this page? Perhaps nothing intentional, perhaps an idle editor found himself with four agency dispatches and thought it was a good idea to run them together to produce a stronger effect. But in fact the newspaper is transmitting an idea, an alarm signal, a warning . . . And in any case, think of the reader: each of these news items, taken individually, would have had little impact, but together they force the reader to stay on that page. Understood? I know it's commonly said that if a laborer attacks a fellow worker, then the newspapers say where he comes from if he's a southerner but not if he comes from the North. All right, that's racism. But imagine a page on which a laborer from Cuneo, etc. etc., a pensioner from Mestre kills his wife, a news vendor from Bologna commits suicide, a builder from Genoa signs a bogus check. What interest is that to readers in the areas where these people were born? Whereas if we're talking about a laborer from Calabria, a pensioner from Matera, a news vendor from Foggia, and a builder from Palermo, then it creates concern about criminals coming up from the South, and this makes news . . . We're a newspaper to be published in Milan, not down in Catania, and we have to bear in mind the feelings of readers in Milan. Note that 'making news' is a great expression. We're the ones who make the news, and we must know how to make it emerge between the lines. Dottor Colonna, you'll spend your free hours with our news team, looking through the agency dispatches, building up pages around a theme, learning to create news where there wasn't any, or where it wasn't to be seen. All right?"

Another topic was the Denial. We were still a newspaper without any readers, and so there was no one to challenge any of the news that we provided. But a newspaper is also judged by its capacity to handle denials, especially if it's a newspaper that shows it doesn't mind getting its hands dirty. Also, by training ourselves for the real denials when they came, we could invent letters from readers that we follow up with a denial. Just to let the Commendatore see what we are capable of.

"I discussed this yesterday with Dottor Colonna. And Colonna would like to give you a little talk on the technique of denial."

"So," I began, "let's give a textbook example, which is not only fictitious but also, let's say, rather far-fetched: a letter-of-denial parody that appeared a few years go in *L'Espresso.* The assumption was that the magazine had heard from a certain Signor Preciso Perniketti as follows."

Dear Editor:

With reference to your article "Ides Murder Suspect Denies All" by Veruccio Veriti, which appeared in the last issue of your magazine, please allow me to correct the following matters. It is not true that I was present at the assassination of Julius Caesar. Please kindly note from the enclosed birth certificate that I was born at Molfetta on March 15, 1944, many centuries after the regrettable event, which moreover I have always deplored. Signor Veriti must have misunderstood me when I told him I invariably celebrate March 15, 1944, with a few friends. It is likewise incorrect that I later told a certain Brutus: "We will meet again at Philippi." I wish to state that I have never had any dealings with anyone called Brutus, whose name I heard for the first time yesterday. During the course of our brief telephone interview, I did indeed tell Signor Veriti that I would soon be meeting the city's assistant traffic officer, Signor Philippi, but the statement was made in the context of a conversation about the circulation of automobile traffic. In this context, I never said that I had appointed assassins to get rid of that traitorous bully Julius Caesar, but rather, "I had an appointment with the assistant traffic officer to get rid of traffic in Boulevard Julius Caesar."

Yours faithfully,
Preciso Perniketti

"How do you deal with such a clear denial without losing face? Here's a good way of replying."

I note that Signor Perniketti does indeed not deny that Julius Caesar was assassinated on the ides of March of '44. I also note that Signor Perniketti always celebrates the anniversary of March 15, 1944, with friends. It was this most curious practice that I wished to report in my article. Signor Perniketti may well have personal reasons for celebrating that date with copious libations, but he will no doubt agree that the coincidence is, to say the least, strange. He will furthermore recall that, during the long and detailed telephone interview with me, he stated, "I believe one should always render unto Caesar that which is Caesar's." A source close to Signor Perniketti—which I have no reason to doubt—has assured me that that which was rendered unto Caesar was twenty-three stab wounds. And I note that Signor Perniketti is careful throughout to avoid telling us who actually inflicted those stab wounds.

As for the pitiful denial about Philippi, I have my notebook in front of me where it is clearly recorded that Signor Perniketti did not say "We will meet again at Philippi's office" but "We will meet again at Philippi."

I can give the same assurance regarding words threatening to Julius Caesar. The notes in my notebook, which I have before me, distinctly say, "appt ass. t. o. get rid of tr. bl. Julius Caesar." These attempts to show that black is white and to play around with words are no way to avoid such weighty responsibility, or to gag the press.

"It is signed by Veruccio Veriti. So, what's the point of this denial of a denial? Point number one, that the newspaper has received the information from sources close to Signor Perniketti. This always works. The sources aren't given, but it implies the newspaper has confidential sources, perhaps more reliable than Perniketti. Use is then made of the journalist's notebook. No one will ever see the notebook, but the idea of an actual record tends to inspire confidence in the newspaper and suggests that there is evidence. Lastly, insinuations are made that are meaningless in themselves but throw a shadow of suspicion over Perniketti. Now, I don't say all denials have to take this form—this is just a parody—but keep in mind the three fundamental elements for a denial of a denial: other sources, notes in the reporter's notebook, and doubts about the reliability of the person making the denial. Understood?"

"Very good," they replied in chorus. And the following day, each brought examples of rather more credible denials, along with denials of denials less grotesque but equally effective. My five students had understood the lesson.

Maia Fresia proposed: "'We take note of the denial but point out that what we have reported appears in the official record of the investigating magistrates, namely in the preliminary notification to the accused.' What readers don't know is that the magistrates then decided not to proceed against Perniketti. They don't know that the official record was a confidential document, nor is it clear how it was obtained, or how genuine it was. I've done what you asked, Dottor Simei, but if you'll allow me, this seems a pretty lousy trick."

"My dear," replied Simei, "it would be even more lousy for the newspaper to admit it hadn't checked its sources. But I agree that rather than giving out information someone would be able to check, it's better to limit yourself to insinuation. Insinuation doesn't involve saying anything in particular, it just serves to raise a doubt about the person making the denial. For example: 'We are happy to note the explanation, but we understand that Signor Perniketti'—always keep to Signor, rather than Onorevole or Dottor; Signor is the worst insult in our country—'has sent dozens of denials to countless newspapers. This must indeed be a full-time compulsion.' This way, readers become convinced he is paranoid. You see the advantage of insinuation: by saying that Perniketti has written to other newspapers, we are simply telling the truth, which can't be denied. The most effective insinuation is the one that gives facts that are valueless in themselves, yet cannot be denied because they are true."

With these recommendations clear in our minds, we began what Simei termed a brainstorming session. Palatino reminded us that he had previously worked on a puzzle magazine, and he suggested the newspaper include half a page of games, along with television schedules, weather, and horoscopes.

"Horoscopes, of course!" Simei said. "Great that you reminded us, they're the first things our readers will be looking for! Yes, of course, this is your first task, Signorina Fresia. Go read a few newspapers and magazines that publish horoscopes, and take some of the recurring themes. But keep to optimistic predictions—people don't like being told that next month they're going to die of cancer. And give predictions that will apply to everyone, by which I mean that a woman of sixty isn't going to be interested in the prospect of meeting the young man of her life, whereas the prediction, let's say, that some event in the coming months will bring this Capricorn lasting happiness will suit everybody—adolescents (if they ever read it), aging spinsters, and office clerks waiting for a pay raise. But let's address the games, my dear Palatino. What do you suggest? Crosswords?"

"Yes, crosswords," said Palatino. "Unfortunately, we have to do the kinds of crosswords that ask who ruled Germany during the Second World War."

"It would be a small miracle if the reader were to write 'Hitler,'" sneered Simei.

"Meanwhile the cryptic crosswords in foreign newspapers have clues that are a puzzle in themselves. Recently, in a French newspaper, I saw 'the friend of simples,' and the solution was 'herbalist,' because simples aren't just simpletons, but also medicinal herbs."

"That's no use to us," said Simei. "Our readers won't know what simples are, nor will they know what an herbalist is or does. Stick with Hitler, or the husband of Eve, or the mother of a calf, and stuff like that."

Maia spoke at this point, her face illuminated by an almost childlike smile, as if she were about to do something mischievous. Crosswords were fine, she said, but readers had to wait for the next issue to find out whether their answers were correct. We could also pretend that some kind of competition had been started in previous issues and the readers' funniest answers could be published here. We could ask readers to provide the silliest answers to an equally silly question.

"At university we amused ourselves by thinking up some weird questions and answers. Like: Why do bananas grow on trees? Because if they grew on the ground, they'd be snapped up by the crocodiles. Why do skis slide on the snow? Because if they slid only on caviar, winter sports would be too expensive."

I joined in the game: "Why was whiskey invented in Scotland? Because if it had been invented in Japan, it would be sake, and you couldn't drink it with soda. Why is the sea so vast? Because there are too many fish, and it would make no sense to put them on the Great Saint Bernard Pass. Why does the rooster crow a hundred and fifty times? Because if it crowed thirty-three times, it would be the Grand Master of the Freemasons."

"Hold on," said Palatino. "Why are glasses open at the top and closed at the bottom? Because if it were the other way around, then bars would go bankrupt. Why do fingernails grow and teeth not? Because otherwise people would bite their teeth when they were nervous. Why do legs bend inward and not out? Because on airplanes it would make forced landings extremely dangerous. Why did Christopher Columbus sail west? Because if he'd sailed east, he would have discovered Naples. Why do fingers have nails? Because if they had pupils, they'd be eyes."

The competition was now in full flow, and Fresia intervened once more: "Why are aspirins different from iguanas? Because have you tried swallowing an iguana?"

"That's enough," said Simei. "This is schoolboy stuff. Don't forget, our readers aren't intellectuals. They haven't read about the surrealists, who used to make exquisite corpses, as they called them. Our readers would take it all seriously and think we were mad. Come on, we're fooling around, we have work to do."

And so the silly-question column was rejected. Too bad, it would have been fun. But this whole business had drawn Maia Fresia to my attention. Along with such wit she must have had a certain charm. And in her own way, she did. Why in her own way? I still wasn't quite sure in what way, but I was curious.

She was obviously feeling frustrated, however, and tried to suggest something more in line with her own interests. "The Strega literary prize is coming up," she said. "Shouldn't we be talking about the books on the shortlist?"

"Always going on about culture, you young people. It's a good thing you didn't graduate, otherwise you'd be suggesting a fifty-page critical essay—"

"No, I didn't graduate, but I do read."

"We can't get too involved in culture, our readers don't read books. The most they're going to read is *La Gazzetta dello Sport.* But I agree, the newspaper will have to have a page, not just on culture, but culture and entertainment. Forthcoming cultural events, however, should be reported in the form of interviews. An interview with the author is reassuring: no authors will speak badly of their books, so our readers will not be exposed to any spiteful or supercilious attacks. Then a lot depends on the questions: you shouldn't talk too much about the book but rather concentrate on the writer, perhaps on his or her foibles and weaknesses. Signorina Fresia, you have experience with celebrity romances. Think of an interview with one of the short-listed authors. If the story is about love, get the author to describe their first love affair, and perhaps to throw a little mud at the other candidates. Turn the wretched book into something human that even a housewife will understand, so she has no regrets if she doesn't read it, and anyway, who reads books that newspapers review? Generally speaking, not even the reviewer. We should be thankful if the book has been read by the author."

"My God," said Maia Fresia, turning pale, "I'll never rid myself of the curse of celebrity romance."

"You haven't exactly been called here to write articles on the economy and international politics."

"I guessed as much. Though I'd hoped I was wrong."

"There now, don't take it badly. Try to put something down, we all have great faith in you."

6

Wednesday, April 15

One morning, I remember Cambria saying: "I heard on the radio that research has shown how air pollution is affecting penis size among the younger generation, and I decided that the problem doesn't relate just to sons, but also to fathers, who are forever boasting about the size of their son's willy. When mine was born and they took me into the room at the hospital where all the newborns were on display, I remember commenting what a fine pair of balls he had, and subsequently boasted to colleagues."

"All newborn boys have enormous testicles," said Simei, "and all fathers say the same thing. And then you know how labels are often mixed up, so perhaps that wasn't your son after all—with the greatest respect to your wife."

"But this news relates to fathers in particular, since there are also said to be harmful effects on the reproductive system of adults," retorted Cambria. "If the idea spreads that pollution is affecting not just whales but also willies, I think we might witness sudden conversions to environmentalism."

"Interesting," commented Simei, "but who is suggesting that the Commendatore, or at least his circle, is concerned about reducing air pollution?"

"But it would raise the alarm, wouldn't it, and quite rightly," said Cambria.

"Maybe, but we're not alarmists," replied Simei. "That would be terrorism—you don't want to start raising doubts over our gas pipeline, our petroleum, our iron and steel industries, do you? We're not the Green Party newspaper. Our readers have to be reassured, not alarmed." Then, after a moment's reflection, he added: "Unless of course the things that affect the penis are produced by a pharmaceutical company, which the Commendatore wouldn't mind alarming. But they're matters to be discussed case by case. In any event, let me know if you have an idea, then I'll decide whether or not to pursue it."

The next day Lucidi arrived at the office with an article practically already written. The story was this. An acquaintance of his had received a letter from the Ordre Souverain Militaire de Saint-Jean de Jérusalem–Chevaliers de Malte–Prieuré Oecuménique de la Sainte-Trinité-de-Villedieu–Quartier Général de la Vallette–Prieuré de Québec, inviting him to become a knight of Malta, subject to a generous reimbursement for a framed diploma, medallion, badge, and other trinkets. Lucidi had decided to investigate the whole business of knightly orders and had made some extraordinary discoveries.

"Listen to this. I've dug up a police report—don't ask me

how—on various fake orders of Malta. There are sixteen of them, not to be confused with the genuine Sovereign Military Hospitaller Order of Saint John of Jerusalem of Rhodes and of Malta, which is based in Rome. Each has more or less the same name with minimal variations. They all alternately recognize, then disown, one another. In 1908 some Russians establish an order in the United States, which in recent years has been led by His Royal Highness Prince Roberto Paternò Ayerbe Aragona, Duke of Perpignan, head of the Royal House of Aragon, claimant to the throne of Aragon and the Balearics, Grand Master of the Orders of the Collar of Saint Agatha of Paternò and of the Royal Balearic Crown. But a Dane breaks away from this branch in 1934 and sets up another order, proclaiming Prince Peter of Greece and Denmark as its chancellor. In the 1960s, a defector from the Russian branch, Paul de Granier de Cassagnac, establishes an order in France and chooses the ex-king of Yugoslavia, Peter II, as its protector. In 1965 ex-king Peter II of Yugoslavia falls out with Cassagnac and founds another order, in New York, of which Prince Peter of Greece and Denmark becomes Grand Prior. In 1966 a certain Robert Bassaraba von Brancovan Khimchiacvili appears as chancellor, though he is expelled and goes off to found the Order of the Ecumenical Knights of Malta, of which Prince Enrico III Costantino di Vigo Lascaris Aleramico Paleologo del Monferrato would become Imperial and Royal Protector. This prince describes himself as heir to the throne of Byzantium, Prince of Thessaly, and would then found another order in Malta. I then find a Byzantine protectorate, created by Prince Carol of Romania, who had broken away from Cassagnac's order; a Grand Priory of which a certain Tonna-Barthet is the Grand Bailiff, while Prince Andrew of Yugoslavia—former Grand Master of the order founded by Peter II—is Grand Master of the Priory of Russia (which would then become Grand Royal Priory of Malta and of Europe). There's even an order created in the 1970s by a Baron de Choibert and by Vittorio Busa, otherwise known as Viktor Timur II, Metropolitan Orthodox Archbishop of Bialystok, Patriarch of the Western and Eastern Diaspora, President of the Democratic Republic of Byelorussia and Gran Khan of Tartary and Mongolia. And then there's an International Grand Priory created in 1971 by the aforementioned Royal Highness Roberto Paternò with the Baron Marquis of Alaro, of which another Paternò would become Grand Protector in 1982—a certain Leopardi Tomassini Paternò of Constantinople, head of the imperial dynasty and heir to the Eastern Roman Empire, consecrated legitimate successor of the Apostolic Catholic Orthodox Church of the Byzantine Rite, Marquis of Monteaperto and Count Palatine of the throne of Poland. In 1971 the Ordre Souverain Militaire de Saint-Jean de Jérusalem appears in Malta (the one from which I started), from a split with that of Bassaraba, under the supreme protection of Alessandro Licastro Grimaldi Lascaris Comneno Ventimiglia, Duke of La Chastre, Sovereign Prince and Marquis of Déols, and its Grand Master is now the Marquis Carlo Stivala of Flavigny, who, on Licastro's death, joins up with Pierre Pasleau, who assumes Licastro's titles, as well as those of His Holiness the Archbishop Patriarch of the Catholic Orthodox Church of Belgium, Grand Master of the Sovereign Military Order of the Temple of Jerusalem and Grand Master and Hierophant of the Universal Masonic Order of the Ancient Oriental Rite and the Joint Primitive Rite of Memphis and Misraim. I forgot to mention that to be *à la page* one could become a member of the Priory of Sion, as a descendant of Jesus Christ, who married Mary Magdalene and founded the Merovingian dynasty."

"The names of these characters are enough in themselves to make news," said Simei, who had been taking notes enthusiastically. "Just think, Paul de Granier de Cassagnac, Licastro (what did you say?) Grimaldi Lascaris Comneno Ventimiglia, Carlo Stivala of Flavigny . . ."

". . . Robert Bassaraba von Brancovan Khimchiacvili," Lucidi repeated jubilantly.

"I think quite a number of our readers will have been taken in by propositions of this kind," I added. "We can help protect them from these opportunists."

Simei hesitated for a moment and said he would give it some thought. The following day he had evidently done some research and told us that our proprietor had received the title of Commendatore from the Order of Saint Mary of Bethlehem: "It turns out that the Order of Saint Mary of Bethlehem was another fake order. The real one was that of Saint Mary of Jerusalem, the Ordo Fratrum Domus Hospitalis Sanctae Mariae Teutonicorum in Jerusalem. It is recognized by the *Pontifical Yearbook,* though I certainly wouldn't place my trust in that, with all that's been going on in the Vatican, but in any event a Commendatore of the Order of Saint Mary of Bethlehem is worth about as little as that of the Mayor of Cockaigne. And do you really want to publish an article that throws a shadow of doubt, even ridicule, on the title of our Commendatore? Each to his own delusion. I'm sorry, Lucidi, but we'll have to scrap your fine article."

"You're saying we have to check whether or not the Commendatore is going to like each article?" asked Cambria, our specialist in stupid questions.

"Of course," replied Simei. "He's our majority shareholder, as they say."

At this point Maia plucked up the courage to mention a possible line of investigation. The story was this. In the Porta Ticinese district, in a part of the city that was becoming increasingly popular with tourists, there was a restaurant and pizzeria called Paglia e Fieno. Maia, who lives by the canals, has been walking past it for years. And for years this vast restaurant, through whose windows you could glimpse at least a hundred seats, was always depressingly empty, except for a few tourists drinking coffee at the tables outside. And it wasn't as if the place was abandoned. Maia had once been inside, out of curiosity, and was alone, except for a small family group twenty tables farther down. She had ordered a dish of *paglia e fieno,* of course, with a quarter liter of white wine and some apple tart, all excellent fare and reasonably priced, with extremely polite waiters. Now, if someone runs premises as vast as that, with staff, kitchen, and so forth, and no one goes there for years, if they had any sense they would sell it off. And yet Paglia e Fieno has been open for maybe ten years, pretty well three hundred and sixty-five days a year.

"There's something strange going on there," observed Costanza.

"Not really," replied Maia. "The explanation is obvious. It's a place owned by the triads, or the Mafia, or the Camorra. It's been bought with dirty money and it's a good, upfront investment. But, you say, the investment is already there, it's in the value of the building, and they could keep it shut down, without putting any more money into it. And yet no—it's open and running. Why?"

"Yes, why?" asked Cambria again.

Her reply revealed that Maia had a smart little brain. "The premises are used, day in day out, for laundering dirty money that's constantly flowing in. You serve the few customers who turn up each evening, but each evening you ring up a series of false till receipts as though you'd had a hundred customers. Once you've registered that amount, you take it to the bank —and perhaps, so as not to attract attention to all that cash, since no one's paying by credit card, you open accounts in twenty different banks. On this sum, which is now legal, you pay all the necessary taxes, after generous deductions for operating expenses and supplies (it's not hard to get false invoices). It's well known that for money laundering you have to count on losing fifty percent. With this system, you lose much less."

"But how do you prove all this?" asked Palatino.

"Simple," replied Maia. "Two revenue officers go there for dinner, a man and woman, looking like newlyweds, and as they're eating they look around and see there are, let's say, just two other customers. Next day the police go and check, find that a hundred till receipts have been rung up, and I'd like to see what those people will have to say for themselves."

"It's not so simple," I pointed out. "The two revenue officers go there, say, at eight o'clock, but however much they eat, they will have to leave by nine, otherwise they'll look suspicious. Who can prove that the hundred customers weren't there between nine and midnight? You then have to send at least three or four couples to cover the evening. Now, if they do a check the next morning, what's going to happen? The police are thrilled to find someone's been underdeclaring, but what can they do with someone who's declaring too much? The restaurant can always say the machine got stuck, that it kept printing out the same thing. And what then? A second check? They're not stupid, they've now figured out who the officers are, and when they come back they won't ring up any false till receipts that evening. Or the police have to keep checking night after night, sending out half an army to eat pizzas, and perhaps after a year they'd manage to close them down, but it's just as likely they'd get bored well before that, because they've got other things to do."

"That's for the police to decide," Maia replied resentfully. "They'll find some clever way—we just have to point out the problem."

"My dear," said Simei affably, "I'll tell you what will happen if we cover this investigation. First, we'll have the police on our backs, as you'll be criticizing them for failing to detect the fraud—and they know how to get their revenge, if not against us then certainly against the Commendatore. And as you say yourself, we have the triads, the Camorra, the 'Ndrangheta, or whoever else, and you think they're going to be pleased? And do we sit here as good as gold, waiting for them to bomb our offices? Finally, you know what I say?

That our readers will be thrilled to eat a good cheap meal in a place that comes straight out of a detective story, so that Paglia e Fieno will be packed with morons and our only accomplishment will be that we've made them a fortune. So we can forget that one. Don't you worry, just go back to your horoscopes."

7

Wednesday, April 15, Evening

I COULD SEE HOW DISPIRITED Maia was, and I caught up with her as she was leaving. Instinctively I took her by the arm.

"Don't take it personally, Maia. Let's go, I'll walk you home. We could have a drink on the way."

"I live by the canals, plenty of bars around there. There's one I know that does an excellent Bellini, my great passion. Thanks."

We reached Ripa Ticinese, and I saw the canals for the first time. I'd heard about them, of course, but was convinced they were all underground, and yet it felt as if we were in Amsterdam. Maia told me with a certain pride that Milan had once been very much like Amsterdam, crisscrossed by canals right to the center. It must have been beautiful, which was why Stendhal had so liked it. But later they had covered the canals for public health reasons, and only here were they still visible, with their putrid water, though at one time there were washerwomen along the banks. And in some of the side streets you could still see rows of old houses and many *case di ringhiera.*

Case di ringhiera, large old buildings with an inner courtyard and iron railings circling the upper floors. They were places I'd heard about, images of the 1950s that I'd come across when editing encyclopedias or when referring to the performance of Bertolazzi's *El Nost Milan* at the Piccolo Teatro. But I didn't imagine any still existed.

Maia laughed. "Milan is full of *case di ringhiera,* except that they're no longer for poor people. Come, I'll show you." She took me into a double courtyard. "Here on the ground floor it's been completely redeveloped. There are workshops for small antiques dealers—though really just glorified junk shops charging high prices—and the studios of painters in search of fame. Now it's all stuff for tourists. But up there, those two floors are exactly as they used to be."

I could see the iron railings around the upper floors, and doors that opened onto each balcony, and I asked whether anyone still hung their wash out to dry.

Maia smiled. "We're not in Naples. Almost all of it has been renovated. At one time the steps went straight up to the balcony, which led to each front door, and at the far end was a single toilet for several families, with a hole in the floor, and you could forget any idea of a shower or a bath. Now it has all been done up for the rich. Some apartments even have a Jacuzzi and they cost an arm and a leg. Less where I live. I've got two rooms with water dripping down the walls, though fortunately they've put in a toilet and a shower, but I love the area. Soon, of course, they'll be fixing that up as well. Then

I'll have to move out, I won't be able to afford the rent, unless *Domani* gets going pretty soon and they take me on permanently. That's why I put up with all this humiliation."

"Don't take it personally, Maia. It's obvious that during a trial period we have to learn what we can write and what we can't. In any event, Simei has responsibilities, to the paper and to the publisher. Perhaps you could do as you liked when you worked on celebrity romance, but here it's different, we're working on a newspaper."

"And that's why I was hoping to get away from all that celebrity garbage, I wanted to be a serious journalist. But perhaps I'm a failure. I never graduated, I had to help my parents, then they died, and it was too late to go back. I'm living in a hole. I'll never be the special correspondent covering the Gulf War . . . What am I doing? Horoscopes, taking advantage of suckers. Isn't that failure?"

"We've only just started. There'll be opportunities for someone like you as soon as we've launched. You've come up with some brilliant ideas. I liked them, and I think Simei liked them too."

I could feel I was lying to her. I should have told her that she was walking into a blind alley, that they'd never send her off to the Gulf, that perhaps it would be better for her to get out before it was too late. But I couldn't depress her any further. I decided instead to tell her the truth, not about her but about me.

And since I was about to bare my soul, like a poet, I adopted a more intimate tone, almost without realizing it.

"Look at me, Maia, see me as I am. I didn't get a degree either. All my life I've done occasional jobs, and now I've ended up past the age of fifty at a newspaper. But you know when I really began to be a loser? When I started thinking of myself as a loser. If I hadn't spent my time brooding about it, I would have won at least one round."

"Past fifty? You don't look it, I mean . . . you don't."

"You'd have said I was only fifty?"

"No, I'm sorry, you're a fine man, and you have a sense of humor. Which is a sign of freshness, youth . . ."

"If anything, it's a sign of wisdom, and therefore of old age."

"No, you obviously don't believe what you're saying, but it's clear you've decided to go along with this venture and you're doing it . . . with cheerful cynicism."

Cheerful? She was a blend of cheer and melancholy and was watching me with the eyes (how would a bad writer have put it?) of a fawn.

Of a fawn? Ah, well . . . it's just that, as we were walking, she looked up at me because I was taller than she was. And that was it. Any woman who looks at you from below looks like Bambi.

Meanwhile we arrived at her bar. She was sipping her Bellini and I felt relaxed in front of my whiskey. I was gazing once again at a woman who wasn't a prostitute, and I felt younger.

Perhaps it was the alcohol . . . I was beginning to feel the urge to confide. When did I last confide in anyone? I told her I'd once had a wife who had walked out on me. I told her I had won that woman over because, at the beginning, I'd messed something up and apologized, said that perhaps

I was stupid. I love you even if you're stupid, she'd told me —things like that can drive you mad with love. But then perhaps she realized I was more stupid than she could handle, and it ended.

Maia laughed. ("What a nice thing to say, I love you even if you're stupid!") And then she told me that even though she was younger and had never thought of herself as stupid, she too had had some unhappy affairs, perhaps because she couldn't bear the stupidity of the other person, or perhaps because most of those roughly her own age seemed so immature. "As if I were the mature one. And so, you see, I'm almost thirty and still on the shelf. It's just that we're never satisfied with what we have."

Thirty? In Balzac's time a woman of thirty was old and wrinkled, and Maia seemed like twenty, apart from a few fine lines around the eyes, as if she had done a lot of crying, or was sensitive to the light and always squinted on sunny days.

"There's nothing better," I said, "than an amiable encounter between two losers," and as soon as I said it, I felt afraid.

"Fool," she said lightly, then she apologized, fearing she had been overly familiar.

"No, on the contrary, thank you," I said. "No one has ever called me fool in such a seductive way."

I had gone too far. Fortunately, she was quick to change the subject. "They're trying to make it look like Harry's Bar," she said, "and they can't even get the spirits in the right place. You see, among the various whiskeys there's a Gordon's gin, and the Sapphire and the Tanqueray are on the other side."

"What, where?" I asked, looking straight ahead, and all

I could see was tables. "No," she said, "at the bar, look." I turned, and she was right, but how could she have imagined I'd seen what she was looking at? At the time I didn't take much notice, and took the opportunity to call for the check. I gave her a few more words of reassurance as I walked her to a door, from which you could see a courtyard and the workshop of a mattress maker. There were still a few mattress makers left, it seemed, despite the television ads for spring mattresses. She thanked me, she smiled, she offered me her hand. It was warm and appreciative.

I returned home along the canals of a benign old Milan. I ought to have been more familiar with the city that held so many surprises.

8

Friday, April 17

Over the next few days, as we were doing our homework (as we now called it), Simei entertained us with projects that were perhaps not pressing, but still demanded our attention.

"I'm not yet sure whether it will be for issue 0/1 or 0/2, though we still have many blank pages for 0/1, and I'm not saying we have to start off with sixty pages like the *Corriere,* but we need at least twenty-four. For some pages, we can get by with advertising. That no one has yet taken any is neither here nor there: we'll lift it from other newspapers and run it as if—and in the meantime it'll inspire confidence in our proprietor, give him a sense of a decent future income."

"And a column with death notices," suggested Maia. "They also bring in cash. Let me make up a few. I love killing off characters with strange names and bereft families, especially the important ones. I like the ones who grieve on the sidelines, those who don't care much about the deceased or the family but use the announcement to name-drop, just so they can say they knew him too."

Sharp as ever. But after our walk of a few evenings ago, I was keeping some distance from her, and she likewise, both of us feeling vulnerable.

"Death notices are fine," said Simei, "but first the horoscopes. I was thinking of something else, though. I mean brothels, or rather, the old-fashioned 'houses of tolerance.' People talk of bordellos even if they have no idea what they are, but I can remember them. I was already an adult in 1958 when they were closed down."

"I too had come of age by then," said Braggadocio. "I explored a few myself."

"I'm not talking about the one in Via Chiaravalle—that was a real bordello, with urinals at the entrance so that troops could relieve themselves before going in—"

"—and shapeless swaggering whores sticking their tongues out at the soldiers and timid provincial lads, and the *maîtresse* shouting, 'Come on, boys, what are we waiting for?'"

"Please, Braggadocio, there's a young lady here."

"Perhaps, if you have to write about it," said Maia, unabashed, "you should say, 'Ripe in years, they strolled indolently, gestured lasciviously, before clients hot with desire.'"

"Well done, Fresia, not exactly like that, but a more delicate language needs to be found. Not least because I was particularly interested in the more respectable houses, such as the one in San Giovanni sul Muro, all Art Nouveau style, full of intellectuals who went there (so they said) in search not of sex but of art history."

"Or the one in Via Fiori Chiari, Art Deco with multicolored tiles," said Braggadocio, his voice full of nostalgia. "Who knows whether our readers recall them."

"And those not yet old enough would have seen them in Fellini films," I added, because when you have no recollections of events, you take them from art.

"I leave that to you, Braggadocio," concluded Simei. "Do me a nice colorful piece saying something along the lines that the good old days weren't so bad after all."

"But why this renewed interest in brothels?" I asked. "It might excite older men, but it would scandalize older women."

"I'll tell you something, Colonna," said Simei. "The old brothel in Via Fiori Chiari closed down in 1958, then someone bought it in the early 1960s and turned it into a restaurant that was very chic with all those multicolored tiles. But they kept one or two cubicles and gilded the bidets. And you've no idea how many women asked their husbands to take them into those cubbyholes to find out what happened in the old days . . . That, of course, only went on until the wives lost interest, or else the food wasn't up to snuff. The restaurant closed, end of story. But listen, I'm thinking of a page with Braggadocio's piece on the left and, on the right, a report on decay in the city's suburbs, with the indecent traffic of young women walking the streets so children can't go out at night. No comment to link the two phenomena, we'll let readers draw their own conclusions. After all, everyone agrees deep down that the houses of tolerance should be brought back—the wives so that husbands will not go around the streets picking up hookers who stink up the car with cheap perfume, the men so they can sneak off into one of those courtyards and, if spotted, they can say they're there to admire the local color. Who will do me the report on hookers?"

Costanza said he would like to do it, and everyone agreed. To spend a few nights driving around the streets was too heavy on gas, and then there was always the risk of bumping into a police patrol.

That evening I was struck by Maia's expression. As if she'd realized she had fallen into a snake pit. And so I waited for her to leave, hung around for a few minutes on the pavement, and then—knowing which route she took—caught up with her halfway home. "I'm leaving, I'm leaving," she said, almost in tears, trembling. "What kind of newspaper have I ended up in? At least my celebrity romances did no harm to anyone—they even brought some business to ladies' hairdressers."

"Maia, don't decide anything yet, Simei is still working things out, we can't be sure he really wants to publish all that stuff. We're still at the drawing board, inventing ideas, possible scenarios, that's a good thing, and nobody has asked you to go around the streets dressed as a hooker to interview anyone. This evening you're looking at it all the wrong way, you've got to stop imagining things. How about going to a movie?"

"Over there is a film I've already seen."

"Over where?"

"Where we just passed on the other side of the street."

"But I was holding your arm and looking at you, I wasn't looking at the other side of the street. You're a strange one."

"You never see the things I see," she said. "Anyway, let's buy a newspaper and see what's playing in the area."

We saw a film of which I remember nothing. Feeling her still trembling, I eventually took her hand, warm and appreciative once more, and we remained there like two young lovers, except that we were like the lovers from the Round Table who slept with a sword between them.

Taking her home—she now seemed a little more cheerful—I kissed her on the forehead, patting her on the cheek as an elderly friend might do. After all, I thought, I could be her father.

Or almost.

9

Friday, April 24

Work went slowly that week. No one seemed eager to do very much, including Simei. On the other hand, twelve issues in a year isn't the same as one a day. I read the first drafts of the articles, tried to give them a uniformity of style and to discourage overly elaborate expressions. Simei approved: "We're doing journalism here, not literature."

"By the way," chipped in Costanza, "this fashion for cell phones is on the increase. Yesterday someone next to me on the train was rambling on about his bank transactions, I learned all about him. People are going crazy. We ought to do a lifestyle piece about it."

"The whole business of cell phones can't last," declared Simei. "First, they cost a fortune and only a few can afford them. Second, people will soon discover it isn't so essential to telephone everyone at all times. They'll lose the enjoyment of private, face-to-face conversation, and at the end of the month they'll discover their phone bill is running out of control. It's a fashion that's going to fizzle out in a year, two at most. Cell phones, for now, are useful only to adulterous husbands, and perhaps plumbers. But no one else. So for our readers, most of whom don't have cell phones, a lifestyle piece is of no interest. And those who have them couldn't care less, or rather, they'd just regard us as snobs, as radical chic."

"Not only that," I said. "Remember that Rockefeller, Agnelli, and the president of the United States don't need cell phones, they have teams of secretaries to look after them. So people will soon realize that only second-raters use them —those poor folk who have to keep in touch with the bank to make sure they're not overdrawn, or with the boss who's checking up on them. And so cell phones will become a symbol of social inferiority, and no one will want them."

"I wouldn't be so sure," said Maia. "It's like prêt-à-porter, or like wearing a T-shirt, jeans, and a scarf: they can be worn just as easily by a woman who's high society or working class, except in the latter case she doesn't know how to match them, or she'll only be seen in brand-new jeans and not those worn at the knee, and she will wear them with high heels, and you can see right away there's nothing stylish about her. But she doesn't know it and happily carries on wearing her ill-matched garments."

"And as she'll be reading *Domani*—we hope—we can tell her she's not a lady. And she has a husband who's second-rate or an adulterer. And there again, perhaps Commendator Vimercate is thinking of checking out cell phone companies, and we'll be doing him a fine service. In short, the question is either irrelevant or too hot to handle. Let's leave it. It's like the business of the computer. Here the Commendatore has given us one each, and they're useful for writing or storing information, though I'm old school and never know what to do with them. Most of our readers are like me and have no use for them because they have no information to store. We'll end up giving our readers inferiority complexes."

Having abandoned the subject of electronics, we set about rereading an article that had been duly corrected, and Braggadocio said, "'Moscow's anger'? Isn't it banal to always use such emphatic expressions—the president's anger, pensioners' rage, and so on and on?"

"No," I said, "these are precisely the expressions readers expect, that's what newspapers have accustomed them to. Readers understand what's going on only if you tell them we're in a no-go situation, the government is forecasting blood and tears, the road is all uphill, the Quirinal Palace is ready for war, Craxi is shooting point-blank, time is pressing, should not be taken for granted, no room for bellyaching, we're in deep water, or better still, we're in the eye of the storm. Politicians don't just say or state emphatically—they roar. And the police act with professionalism."

"Do we really always have to talk about professionalism?" asked Maia. "Everyone here is a professional. A master builder who puts up a wall that hasn't collapsed is certainly acting professionally, but professionalism ought to be the norm, and we should only be talking about the dodgy builder who puts up a wall that does collapse. When I call the plumber and he unblocks the sink, I'm pleased, of course, and I say well done, thanks, but I don't say he acted professionally. And you don't expect him to behave like Joe Piper in the Mickey Mouse story. This insistence on professionalism, that it's something special, makes it sound as if people are generally lousy workers."

"That's the point," I said. "Readers think that people generally *are* lousy workers, which is why we need examples of professionalism—it's a more technical way of saying that everything's gone well. The police have caught the chicken thief—and they've acted with professionalism."

"But it's like calling John XXIII the Good Pope. This presupposes the popes before him were bad."

"Maybe that's what people actually thought, otherwise he wouldn't have been called good. Have you seen a photo of Pius XII? In a James Bond movie he'd have been the head of SPECTRE."

"But it was the newspapers that called John XXIII the Good Pope, and the people followed suit."

"That's right. Newspapers teach people how to think," Simei said.

"But do newspapers follow trends or create trends?"

"They do both, Signorina Fresia. People don't know what the trends are, so we tell them, then they know. But let's not get too involved in philosophy—we're professionals. Carry on, Colonna."

"Good," I said. "Now let me go on with my list. We need to have our cake and eat it, keep our finger on the pulse, take to the field, be in the spotlight, make the best of a bad job.

Once out of the tunnel, once the goose is cooked, nothing gets in our way, we keep our eyes peeled, a needle in a haystack, the tide turns, television takes the lion's share and leaves just the crumbs, we're getting back on track, listening figures have plummeted, give a strong signal, an ear to the ground, emerging in bad shape, at three hundred and sixty degrees, a nasty thorn in the side, the party's over . . . And above all, apologize. The Anglican Church apologizes to Darwin, Virginia apologizes for the ordeal of slavery, the electric company apologizes for the power cuts, the Canadian government officially apologizes to the Inuit people. You mustn't say the Church has revised its original position on the rotation of the Earth but rather that the pope apologizes to Galileo."

Maia clapped her hands and said, "It's true, I could never understand whether this vogue for apologizing is a sign of humility or of impudence: you do something you shouldn't have done, then you apologize and wash your hands of it. It reminds me of the old joke about a cowboy riding across the prairie who hears a voice from heaven telling him to go to Abilene, then at Abilene the voice tells him to go into the saloon and put all his money on number five. Tempted by the voice, he obeys, number eighteen comes up, and the voice murmurs, Too bad, we've lost."

We laughed and then moved on. We had to examine and discuss Lucidi's piece on the events concerning the Pio Albergo Trivulzio, and this took a good half hour. Afterward, in a sudden act of generosity, Simei ordered coffee for everyone from the bar downstairs. Maia, who was sitting between me and Braggadocio, said, "I would do the opposite. I mean, if the newspaper were for a more sophisticated readership, I'd like to do a column that says the opposite."

"That says the opposite of Lucidi?" asked Braggadocio.

"No, no, what are you talking about? I mean the opposite of commonplaces."

"We were talking about that more than half an hour ago," said Braggadocio.

"All right, but I was still thinking about it."

"We weren't," said Braggadocio.

Maia didn't appear to be too upset by the objection and shrugged us off: "I mean the opposite of the eye of the storm or the minister who thunders. For example, Venice is the Amsterdam of the South, sometimes imagination exceeds reality, given that I'm a racist, hard drugs are the first step toward smoking joints, don't make yourself at home, let's stand on ceremony, those who pursue pleasure are always happy, I may be senile but I'm not old, Greek is all math to me, success has gone to my head, Mussolini did a lot of bad after all, Paris is horrid though Parisians are nice, in Rimini everyone stays on the beach and never sets foot in the clubs."

"Yes, and a whole mushroom was poisoned by one family. Where do you get all this garbage?" asked Braggadocio.

"From a book that came out a few months ago," said Maia. "Excuse me, they're no good for *Domani*. No one would ever guess them. Perhaps it's time to go home."

"Listen," Braggadocio muttered to me afterward, "let's go, I'm dying to tell you something."

Half an hour later we were on our way to Taverna Moriggi, though as we walked there Braggadocio mentioned nothing about his revelations. Instead, he said, "You must have noticed that something's wrong with Maia. She's autistic."

"Autistic? But autistic people keep closed up in themselves, don't they? Why do you say she's autistic?"

"I read about an experiment on the early symptoms of autism. Suppose you're in a room with me and Pierino, a child who is autistic. You tell me to hide a small ball and then to leave. I put it into a bowl. Once I've left, you take the ball from the bowl and put it into a drawer. Then you ask Pierino: When Signor Braggadocio returns, where will he look for the ball? And Pierino will say: In the drawer, no? In other words, Pierino won't think that in my mind the ball is still in the bowl, because in his mind it's already in the drawer. Pierino can't put himself in someone else's position, he thinks that everyone is thinking what he's thinking."

"But that's not autism."

"I don't know, perhaps it's a mild form of autism, like touchiness being the first stage of paranoia. But that's how Maia is—she can't see the other person's point of view, she thinks everyone's thinking like her. Didn't you notice the other day, at a certain point she said that he had nothing to do with it, and this 'he' was someone we'd been talking about an hour earlier. She was still thinking about him, or he'd returned to her thoughts at that moment, but it didn't occur to her that we might have stopped thinking about him. She's mad, I tell you. And watch her as she talks, like an oracle—"

This sounded like nonsense and I cut him short: "Those

who play oracles are always mad. Maybe she's descended from the Cumaean Sibyl."

We had reached the tavern. Braggadocio got to the point.

"I've got my hands on a scoop that would sell a hundred thousand copies of *Domani,* if only it was already on sale. In fact, I want some advice. Should I give what I'm investigating to Simei or try to sell it to another newspaper, to a real one? It's dynamite, involves Mussolini."

"It doesn't sound like a story of great topical interest."

"The topical interest is the discovery that someone has been deceiving us, in fact lots of people. In fact, they've all been deceiving us."

"In what sense?"

"A long story. All I have for now is a theory, and with no car I can't get where I have to go to interview the surviving witnesses. Let's start with the facts as we all know them, then I'll tell you why my theory is reasonable."

Braggadocio did no more than summarize what he described as the commonly accepted story, which, according to him, was just too simple to be true.

So, the Allies have broken through the Gothic Line and are moving north toward Milan. The war is now lost, and on April 18, 1945, Mussolini leaves Lake Garda and arrives in Milan, where he takes refuge in the headquarters of the city prefect. He again consults his ministers about possible resistance in a Valtellina fortress. He's now ready for the end. Two days later he gives the last interview of his life to the last of his faithful followers, Gaetano Cabella, who directed the last Fascist newspaper, the *Popolo di Alessandria.* On April 22 he makes his last speech to some officials of the Republican Guard, saying, "If the fatherland is lost, life is not worth living."

Over the next few days the Allies reach Parma, Genoa is liberated, and finally, on the fateful morning of April 25, workers occupy the factories of Sesto San Giovanni. In the afternoon, together with some of his men, including General Graziani, Mussolini is received by Cardinal Schuster at the Archbishop's Palace, where he meets a delegation from the National Liberation Committee. The Liberation Committee demands unconditional surrender, warning that even the Germans have begun negotiating with them. The Fascists (the last are always the most desperate) refuse to accept ignominious surrender, ask for time to think, and leave.

That evening the Resistance leaders can wait no longer for their adversaries to make up their minds, and give the order for a general insurrection. That is when Mussolini escapes toward Como, with a convoy of faithful followers.

His wife, Rachele, has arrived in Como with their son and daughter, Romano and Anna Maria, but inexplicably, Mussolini refuses to meet them.

"Why?" asked Braggadocio. "Was he waiting to meet his mistress? But Claretta Petacci hadn't yet arrived, so what would it have cost him to see his family for ten minutes? Remember this point—it's what first aroused my suspicions."

Mussolini regarded Como as a safe base, as it was said there were few partisans in the vicinity and he could hide there until the Allies arrived. Indeed, Mussolini's real problem was how to avoid falling into the hands of the partisans and to surrender to the Allies, who would have given him a proper trial, then time would tell. Or perhaps he thought that from Como he could get to the Valtellina, where faithful supporters such as Alessandro Pavolini were reassuring him he could organize a powerful resistance with several thousand men.

"But at this point he leaves Como. And try explaining to me the toing and froing of that ill-fated convoy, I can't figure it out either, and for the purposes of my investigation it's of little importance precisely where they come or go. Let's say that they head toward Menaggio, in an attempt to reach Switzerland, then the convoy reaches Cardano, where it's joined by Claretta Petacci, and a German escort appears that has received orders from Hitler to take his friend to Germany (maybe an aircraft would be waiting at Chiavenna to fly him safely to Bavaria). Someone suggests it's not possible to get to Chiavenna, so the convoy returns to Menaggio and, during the night, Pavolini arrives. He is supposed to be bringing military support but has only seven or eight men from the Republican National Guard with him. The Duce feels he is being hunted down and that the only option, rather than resistance in the Valtellina, is for him, along with Fascist Party leaders and their families, to join a German column trying to cross the Alps. There are twenty-eight truckloads of soldiers, with machine guns on each truck, and a column of Italians consisting of an armored car and ten or so civilian vehicles. But at Musso, just before Dongo, the column comes upon men from the Puecher detachment of the 52nd Garibaldi Brigade. There are only a few of them; their commander is known as

'Pedro,' Count Pier Luigi Bellini delle Stelle, and the political commissar is 'Bill,' Urbano Lazzaro. Pedro is impulsive and starts bluffing. He convinces the Germans that the mountainside around them is teeming with partisans and threatens to order the firing of mortars, which in fact are still in German hands. He realizes that the German commandant is attempting to resist, but the soldiers are frightened. All they want is to save their skin and get back home, so he becomes increasingly aggressive. In short, after much shilly-shallying and tiresome negotiations, which I will spare you, Pedro persuades the Germans not only to surrender, but to abandon the Italians who were dragging along behind them. And only in this way could they proceed to Dongo, where they would have to undergo a general search. In short, the Germans treat their allies abominably, but skin is skin."

Pedro asks for the Italians to be handed over to his jurisdiction, not only because he's sure they are Fascist leaders, but also because it's rumored that Mussolini himself might be among them. Pedro is not sure what to think. He negotiates terms with the commander of the armored vehicle, Francesco Barracu, undersecretary to the prime minister (of the defunct Italian Social Republic), a wounded war veteran who boasts a military gold medal and who makes a favorable impression on Pedro. Barracu wants to head for Trieste, where he proposes to save the city from the Yugoslav invasion. Pedro politely suggests he is mad—he would never reach Trieste, and if he did, he would find himself alone against Tito's army—so Barracu asks if he can turn back and rejoin Graziani, God only knows where. In the end, Pedro (having searched the armored vehicle and found no Mussolini) agrees to let them turn around, because he doesn't want to get involved in a skirmish that could draw the Germans back. But as he goes off to deal with another matter, he orders his men to make sure the armored vehicle actually does turn around—should it move even two meters forward they must open fire. What happens then is anyone's guess: either the armored vehicle accelerated forward, shooting, or it was moving ahead simply to turn around and the partisans became nervous and opened fire. There's a brief exchange of shots, two Fascists dead and two partisans wounded. The passengers in the armored vehicle and those in the cars are arrested. Among them Pavolini, who tries to escape by throwing himself into the lake, but he is caught and put back with the others, soaked to the skin.

At this point Pedro receives a message from Bill in Dongo. While they are searching the trucks of the German column, Bill is called over by Giuseppe Negri, a partisan who tells him in dialect, "*Ghè chi el Crapun,*" the big baldhead was there; that is, the strange soldier with the helmet, sunglasses, and greatcoat collar turned up was none other than Mussolini. Bill investigates, the strange soldier plays dumb, but he is finally unmasked. It actually is him, the Duce, and Bill—not sure what to do—tries to measure up to the historic moment and says, "In the name of the Italian people, I arrest you." He takes him to the town hall.

Meanwhile at Musso, in one of the carloads of Italians, there are two women, two children, and a man who claims to be the Spanish consul and has an important meeting in Switzerland with an unspecified British agent. But his papers look false, and he is put under arrest.

Pedro and his men are making history, but don't at first seem aware of it. Their only concern is to keep public order, to prevent a lynching, to reassure the prisoners that not a hair on their heads will be touched, that they will be handed over to the Italian government as soon as arrangements can be made. And indeed, on the afternoon of April 27, Pedro manages to telephone the news of the arrest to Milan, and then the National Liberation Committee comes into the picture. It had just received a telegram from the Allies demanding that the Duce and all members of the Social Republic government be handed over, in accordance with a clause in the armistice signed in 1943 between Badoglio and Eisenhower. ("Benito Mussolini, his chief Fascist associates . . . who now or in the future are in territory controlled by the Allied Military Command or by the Italian Government, will forthwith be apprehended and surrendered into the hands of the United Nations.") And it was said that an aircraft was due to land at Bresso Airport to collect the dictator. The Liberation Committee was convinced that Mussolini, in the hands of the Allies, would have managed to get out alive, perhaps be locked up in a fortress for a few years, then resurface. But Luigi Longo, who represented the Communists on the committee, said that Mussolini had to be done away with summarily, with no trial and with no famous last words. The majority of the committee felt that the country needed an immediate symbol, a concrete symbol, to make it clear that twenty years of fascism really had ended: it needed the dead body of the Duce. And there was a further fear: not just of the Allies getting their hands on Mussolini, but that if Mussolini's fate remained unknown, his image would linger as a bodiless but awkward presence, like the legend of Frederick Barbarossa, closed up in a cave, ready to inspire every fantasy of a return to the past.

"And you'll see in a moment whether those in Milan weren't right . . . Not everyone, however, held the same view: among the members of the Liberation Committee, General Cadorna was in favor of satisfying the Allies, but he was in the minority, and the committee decided to send a mission to Como to execute Mussolini. The patrol—once again, according to the commonly accepted account—was led by a die-hard Communist known as Colonel Valerio and by the political commissar, Aldo Lampredi.

"I'll save you all the alternative versions; for example, that it wasn't Valerio who went to carry it out but someone more important than him. It's even rumored that the real executioner was Matteotti's son, there to avenge his father's assassination, or that the one who pulled the trigger was Lampredi, the mastermind behind the mission. And so on. But let's accept what was disclosed in 1947, that Valerio was the nom de guerre of Walter Audisio, the man who would later become a Communist parliamentary hero. As far as I'm concerned, whether it was Valerio or someone else makes little difference, so let's continue calling him Valerio. Valerio and a group of his men head for Dongo. Pedro, in the meantime, unaware of the imminent arrival of Valerio, decides to hide the Duce, because he fears that Fascist units roaming the area might try to free him. To make sure the prisoner's refuge remains secret, he decides to move him discreetly, of course, but assuming that the news would be passed on, internally, to the customs officials at Germasino. The Duce would have to be taken at night and moved to another place, known only to a handful, toward Como."

At Germasino, Pedro has an opportunity to exchange a few words with the person under arrest, who asks him to send his greetings to a lady who was in the Spanish consul's car, and with some hesitation he admits that she is Claretta Petacci. Pedro would then meet Claretta Petacci, who at first pretends she is someone else, then relents and unburdens herself, talking about her life with the Duce and asking as a last request to be reunited with the man she loves. Pedro is now unsure what to do, but having consulted his companions, he is moved by the story and agrees. This is why Claretta Petacci is there during Mussolini's nighttime transfer to the next place, which in fact they never reach, because news arrives that the Allies have reached Como and are wiping out the last pockets of Fascist opposition; the small convoy of two vehicles therefore heads north once again. The cars stop at Azzano, and after a short distance on foot the fugitives reach the home of the De Maria family—people who can be trusted—and Mussolini and Claretta Petacci are given a small room with a double bed.

Unbeknown to Pedro, this is the last time he will see Mussolini. He returns to Dongo. A truck arrives in the main piazza, full of soldiers wearing brand-new uniforms, quite different from the torn and shabby dress of his partisans. The soldiers line up in front of the town hall. Their leader presents himself as Colonel Valerio, an officer sent with full authority from the general command of the Volunteer Freedom Corps. He produces impeccable credentials and states he has been sent to shoot the prisoners, all of them. Pedro tries to argue, requesting that the prisoners be handed over to those who can carry out a proper trial, but Valerio pulls rank, calls for the list of those arrested, and marks a black cross beside each name. Pedro sees that Claretta Petacci is also to be sentenced to death, and he objects. He says she is only the dictator's lover, but Valerio replies that his orders come from headquarters in Milan.

"And note this point, which emerges clearly from Pedro's account, because in other versions Valerio would say that Claretta Petacci clung to her man, that he had told her to move away, that she had refused and was therefore killed by mistake, so to speak, or through excessive zeal. The thing is that she had already been condemned, but this isn't the point. The truth is, Valerio tells different stories and we can't rely on him."

Various confusing incidents follow. Having been told of the alleged presence of the Spanish consul, Valerio wants to see him, talks to him in Spanish, but the man can't answer, calling into question his Spanish credentials. Valerio gives him a violent slap, identifies him as Vittorio Mussolini, and orders Bill to take him down to the lake and shoot him. But on their way to the lake, someone recognizes him as Marcello Petacci, Claretta's brother, and Bill retrieves him. To no avail. As Marcello jabbers about the services he has done for the fatherland, about secret arms he had found and hidden from Hitler, Valerio adds his name to the list of those condemned to die.

Valerio and his men go straight to the house of the De Maria family, take Mussolini and Petacci, drive them to a lane in Giulino di Mezzegra, where he orders them out. It seems that Mussolini first imagines Valerio has come to free him, and only then does he realize what awaits him. Valerio pushes him against the railings and reads the sentence, trying (he would later say) to separate Mussolini from Claretta, who remains desperately clinging to her lover. Valerio tries to shoot, the machine gun jams, he asks Lampredi for another, and fires five bursts. He would later say that Petacci suddenly moved into the line of fire and was killed by mistake. It's the twenty-eighth of April.

"We know all this from Valerio's account. Mussolini, according to him, ended up as a husk of humanity, though legend would subsequently claim he pulled open his greatcoat shouting, 'Aim for the heart!' No one really knows what happened in that lane apart from the executioners, who would later be manipulated by the Communist Party."

Valerio returns to Dongo and organizes the shooting of all the other Fascist leaders. Barracu asks not to be shot in the back but is shoved into the group. Valerio also puts Marcello Petacci among them, but the other condemned men protest, they regard him as a traitor, and it's anyone's guess what that individual had really been up to. It is then decided to shoot him separately. Once the others have been shot, Petacci breaks free and runs off toward the lake. He's caught but manages to free himself once again, dives into the water, swimming desperately, and is finished off by machine-gun fire and rifle shots. Later Pedro, who refused to let his men take part in the execution, arranges for the corpse to be fished out and put onto the same truck as the others. The truck is dispatched to Giulino to pick up the bodies of the Duce and Claretta. Then off to Milan, where on April 29 they are all dumped in Piazzale Loreto, the same place where the corpses of partisans shot almost a year before had been dumped—the Fascist militia had left them out in the sun for a whole day, preventing the families from collecting the remains.

At this point Braggadocio took my arm, grasping it so firmly that I had to pull away. "Sorry," he said, "but I'm about to reach the core of my problem. Listen carefully. The last time Mussolini was seen in public by people who knew him was the afternoon at the Archbishop's Palace in Milan. From that point on, he traveled only with his closest followers. And from the moment he was picked up by the Germans, then arrested by the partisans, none of those who had dealings with him had known him personally. They had seen him only in photographs or in propaganda films, and the photographs of the last two years showed him so thin and worn that it was rumored he was no longer himself. I told you about the last interview with Cabella, on April 20, which Mussolini checked and signed on the twenty-second, you remember? Well, Cabella notes in his memoirs: 'I immediately observed that Mussolini was in excellent health, contrary to rumors circulating. He was in far better health than the last time I'd seen him. That was in December 1944, on the occasion of his speech at Lirico. On the previous occasions he had received me—in February, in March, and in August of '44—he had never appeared as fit. His complexion was healthy and tanned, his eyes alert, swift in their movements. He had also gained some weight. Or at least he no longer had that leanness that had so struck me in February of the previous year and which gave his face a gaunt, almost emaciated look.'

"Let's admit that Cabella was carrying out a propaganda exercise and wanted to present a Duce in full command of his faculties. Now let's turn to the written account given by Pedro, who describes his first encounter with the Duce after the arrest: 'He's sitting to the right of the door, at a large table. I wouldn't know it's him, wouldn't recognize him, perhaps. He is old, emaciated, scared. He stares, is unable to focus. He jerks his head here and there, looking around as though frightened.' All right, he'd just been arrested, he was bound to be scared, but not a week had passed since the interview, when he was confident he could get across the border. Do you think one man can lose so much weight in seven days? So the man who spoke to Cabella and the man who spoke to Pedro were not one and the same person. Note that not even Valerio knew Mussolini personally. Valerio had gone to execute a legend, an image, to execute the man who harvested corn and proclaimed Italy's entry into the war—"

"You're telling me there were two Mussolinis—"

"Let's move on. News spreads around the city that the corpses have arrived, and Piazzale Loreto is invaded by a loud and angry crowd, who trample on the corpses, disfiguring them, insulting them, spitting on them, kicking them. A woman put five gunshots into Mussolini, one for each of her five sons killed in the war, while another pissed on Claretta Petacci. Eventually someone intervened and hung the dead by the feet from the canopy of a gas station to prevent their being torn to pieces. Here are some photographs—I've cut these out from newspapers of the time. This is Piazzale Loreto and the bodies of Mussolini and Claretta right after a squad of partisans had taken the bodies down the next day and transported them to the mortuary in Piazzale Gorini. Look carefully at these photos. They are bodies of people disfigured, first by bullets, then by brutal trampling. Besides, have you ever seen the face of someone photographed upside down, with the eyes where the mouth should be and the mouth where the eyes should be? The face is unrecognizable."

"So the man in Piazzale Loreto, the man killed by Valerio, was not Mussolini? But Claretta Petacci, when she joined him, she'd have known him perfectly well—"

"We'll come back to Petacci. For now, let me just fill in my theory. A dictator must have a double, who knows how many times he had used him at official parades, seen always from a distance, to avoid assassination attempts. Now imagine that to enable the Duce to escape unhindered, from the moment he leaves for Como, Mussolini is no longer Mussolini but his double."

"And where's Mussolini?"

"Hold on, I'll get to him in good time. The double has lived a sheltered life for years, well paid and well fed, and is put on show only on certain occasions. He now thinks he is Mussolini, and is persuaded to take his place once more—

even if he's captured before crossing the frontier, he is told no one would dare harm the Duce. He should play the part without overdoing it, until the arrival of the Allies. Then he can reveal his identity. He has nothing to be accused of, will get away with a few months in a prison camp at worst. In exchange, a tidy nest egg awaits him in a Swiss bank."

"But the Fascist leaders who are with him to the last?"

"They have accepted the whole setup to allow their leader to escape, and if he reaches the Allies he'll try to save them. Or the more fanatical of them are thinking of a resistance to the very end, and they need a credible image to electrify the last desperate supporters prepared to fight. Or Mussolini, right from the start, has traveled in a car with two or three trusty collaborators, and all the other leaders have always seen him from a distance, wearing sunglasses. I don't know, but it doesn't really make that much difference. The fact is that the double is the only way of explaining why the fake Mussolini avoided being seen by his family at Como.

"And Claretta Petacci?"

"That is the most pathetic part of the story. She arrives expecting to find the Duce, the real one, and someone immediately informs her she has to accept the double as the real Mussolini, to make the story more credible. She has to play the part as far as the frontier, then she'll have her freedom."

"But the whole final scene, where she clings to him and wants to die with him?"

"That's what Colonel Valerio tells us. Let's assume that when the double sees he's being put up against the wall, he shits himself and cries out that he's not Mussolini. What a coward, Valerio would have said, he'll try anything. And he shoots him. Claretta Petacci had no interest in confirming that this man wasn't her lover, and would have embraced him to make the scene more believable. She never imagined that Valerio would have shot her as well, but who knows, women are hysterical by nature, perhaps she lost her head, and Valerio had no choice but to stop her with a burst of gunfire. Or consider this other possibility: Valerio becomes aware it's a double, yet he had been sent to kill Mussolini—he, the sole appointed, of all Italians. Was he to relinquish the glory that awaited him? And so he goes along with the game. If a double looks like his dictator while he's alive, he'll look even more like him once dead. Who could deny it? The Liberation Committee needed a corpse, and they'd have it. If the real Mussolini showed up alive someday, it could always be maintained that he was the double."

"But the real Mussolini?"

"This is the part of the story I still have to figure out. I have to explain how he managed to escape and who had helped him. Broadly speaking, it goes something like this. The Allies don't want Mussolini to be captured by the partisans because he holds secrets that could embarrass them, such as the correspondence with Churchill and God knows what else. And this would be reason enough. But above all, the liberation of Milan marks the beginning of the Cold War. Not only are the Russians approaching Berlin, having conquered half of Europe, but most of the partisans are Communists, heavily armed, and for the Russians they therefore constitute a fifth column ready to hand Italy over to them. And so the Allies, or at least the Americans, have to prepare a possible resistance to a pro-Soviet revolution. To do this, they also need to make use of Fascist veterans. Besides, didn't they save Nazi scientists, such as von Braun, shipping them off to America to prepare for the conquest of space? American secret agents aren't too fussy about such things. Mussolini, once rendered harmless as an enemy, could come in handy tomorrow as a friend. He therefore has to be smuggled out of Italy and, so to speak, put into hibernation for a time."

"And how?"

"But heavens above, who was it that intervened to stop things going too far? The Archbishop of Milan, who was certainly acting on instructions from the Vatican. And who had helped loads of Nazis and Fascists to escape to Argentina? The Vatican. So try to imagine this: on leaving the Archbishop's Palace, they put the double into Mussolini's car, while Mussolini, in another, less conspicuous car, is driven to the Castello Sforzesco."

"Why the castle?"

"Because from the Archbishop's Palace to the castle, if a car cuts along past the cathedral, over Piazza Cordusio, and into Via Dante, it'll reach the castle in five minutes. Easier than going to Como, no? And even today the castle is full of underground passageways. Some are known, and are used for dumping garbage, etc. Others existed for war purposes and became air-raid shelters. Well, many records tell us that in previous centuries there were passageways, actual tunnels, that led from the castle to points in the city. One of these is said to still exist, though the route can no longer be traced due to collapses, and it's supposed to go from the castle to the Convent of Santa Maria delle Grazie. Mussolini is hidden there for several days while everyone searches for him in the North, and then his double is ripped apart in Piazzale Loreto. As soon as things in Milan have calmed down, a vehicle with a Vatican City license plate comes to collect him at night. The roads at the time are in a poor state, but from church to church, monastery to monastery, one eventually reaches Rome. Mussolini vanishes behind the walls of the Vatican, and I'll let you choose the best outcome: either he remains there, perhaps disguised as an old decrepit monsignor, or they put him on a boat for Argentina, posing as a sickly, cantankerous hooded friar with a fine beard and a Vatican passport. And there he waits."

"Waits for what?"

"I'll tell you that later. For the moment, my theory ends here."

"But to develop a theory you need evidence."

"I'll have that in a few days, once I've finished work on various archives and newspapers of the period. Tomorrow is April 25, a fateful date. I'm going to meet someone who knows a great deal about those days. I'll be able to demonstrate that the corpse in Piazzale Loreto was not that of Mussolini."

"But aren't you supposed to be writing the article on the old brothels?"

"Brothels I know from memory, I can dash it off in an hour on Sunday evening. Thanks for listening. I needed to talk to someone."

Once again he let me pay the bill, though this time he'd earned it. We walked out, and he looked around and set off, sticking close to the walls, as though worried about being tailed.

10

Sunday, May 3

BRAGGADOCIO WAS CRAZY. Perhaps he'd made the whole thing up, though it had a good ring to it. But the best part was still to come and I'd just have to wait.

From one madness to another: I hadn't forgotten Maia's alleged autism. I had told myself I wanted to study her mind more closely, but I now knew I wanted something else. That evening I walked her home once again and didn't stop at the main entrance but crossed the courtyard with her. Under a small shelter was a red Fiat 500 in rather poor condition. "It's my Jaguar," said Maia. "It's nearly twenty years old but still runs, it has to be checked over once a year, and there's a local mechanic who has spare parts. I'd need a lot of money to do it up properly, but then it becomes a vintage car and sells at collectors' prices. I use it just to get to Lake Orta. I haven't told you—I'm an heiress. My grandmother left me a small house up in the hills, little more than a hut, I wouldn't get much if I sold it. I've furnished it a little at a time, there's a fireplace, an old black-and-white TV, and from the window you can see the lake and the island of San Giulio. It's my *buen retiro,* I'm there almost every weekend. In fact, do you want to come on Sunday? We'll set off early, I'll prepare a light lunch at midday —I'm not a bad cook—and we'll be back in Milan by suppertime."

On Sunday morning, after we'd been in the car for a while, Maia, who was driving, said, "You see? It's falling to pieces now, but years ago it used to be beautiful red brick."

"What?"

"The road repairman's house, the one we just passed on the left."

"If it was on the left, then only you could have seen it. All I can see from here is what's on the right. This sarcophagus would hardly fit a newborn baby, and to see anything on your left I'd have to lean over you and stick my head out the window. Don't you realize? There's no way I could see that house."

"If you say so," she said, as if I had acted oddly.

At that point I had to explain to her what her problem was.

"Really," she replied with a laugh. "It's just that, well, I now see you as my lord protector and assume you're always thinking what I'm thinking."

I was taken by surprise. I certainly didn't want her to think that I was thinking what she was thinking. That was too intimate.

At the same time I was overcome by a sort of tenderness.

I could feel Maia's vulnerability, she took refuge in an inner world of her own, not wanting to see what was going on in the world of other people, the world that had perhaps hurt her. And yet I was the one in whom she placed her trust, and, unable or unwilling to enter my world, she imagined I could enter hers.

I felt embarrassed when we walked into the house. Pretty, though spartan. It was early May and still cool. She lit a fire, and as soon as it got going, she stood up and looked at me brightly, her face reddened by the first flames: "I'm . . . happy," she said, and that happiness of hers won me over.

"I'm . . . happy too," I said. I took her by the shoulders and kissed her, and felt her take hold of me, thin as a mite. But Braggadocio was wrong: she had breasts, and I could feel them, small but firm. The Song of Songs: like two young fawns.

"I'm happy," she repeated.

I tried to resist: "But I'm old enough to be your father."

"What beautiful incest," she said.

She sat on the bed, and with a flick of a heel and toe, she tossed her shoes across the room. Braggadocio was perhaps right, she was mad, but that gesture forced me to submit.

We skipped lunch. We stayed there in her nest until evening; it didn't occur to us to return to Milan. I was trapped. I felt as if I were twenty or perhaps a mere thirty like her.

"Maia," I said to her the next morning on the way back, "we have to go on working with Simei until I've scraped a little money together, then I'll take you away from that den of vermin. But hold out a little longer. Then, who knows, maybe we'll go off to the South Seas."

"I don't believe it, but it's nice to imagine: Tusitala. For now, if you stay close, I'll even put up with Simei and do the horoscopes."

11

Friday, May 8

On the morning of May 5, Simei seemed excited. "I have a job for one of you—perhaps Palatino, since he's free at the moment. You've read over the past few months—the news was fresh in February—about an examining magistrate who started investigating the state of old people's homes. A real scoop after the case of the Pio Albergo Trivulzio. None of these places belongs to our proprietor, but you know that he owns rest homes, also on the Adriatic coast. It remains to be seen whether sooner or later this magistrate is going to stick his nose into the Commendatore's affairs. Our proprietor would therefore be pleased to see how we might raise a shadow of suspicion over a busybody magistrate. These days, you know, to answer an accusation you don't have to prove it's wrong, all you have to do is undermine the authority of the accuser. So, Palatino, here's the fellow's name. Take a trip down to Rimini with a tape recorder and a camera, and tail this honest and upright servant of the state. No one is one hundred percent upright—he may not be a pedophile, he may not have killed his grandmother or pocketed bribes, but surely there will be something strange about him. Or else, if you'll pardon the expression, you can strangify whatever he does each day. And Palatino, use your imagination. Get it?"

Three days later Palatino came back with some tasty nuggets. He had photographed the magistrate sitting on a park bench, nervously chain-smoking, with ten or so butts at his feet. Palatino wasn't sure whether this could be of any interest, but Simei said yes, a man from whom we expect careful consideration and objectivity was showing signs of being neurotic, and above all a shirker who rather than sweating over files was wandering around in parks. Palatino had also photographed him through the window of a Chinese restaurant while he was eating—and with chopsticks.

"Splendid," said Simei. "Our readers don't go to Chinese restaurants, perhaps there aren't any where they live, and they'd never dream of eating with chopsticks like savages. So why, our readers will ask, is this man hanging around in Chinese restaurants? If he's a serious magistrate, why isn't he eating minestrone or spaghetti like everybody else?"

"Not only that," added Palatino, "he was also wearing colored socks, a sort of emerald or pea green . . . and sneakers."

"Nooo! Sneakers . . . and emerald socks . . . well!" exclaimed Simei jubilantly. "This man's a dandy, or a flower child, as they used to say. And it doesn't take much to picture him smoking joints. Not that you will say this, readers will figure it out for themselves. So, Palatino, work up these details to create a portrait full of dark innuendo, and that will take care of him. Out of a nonstory we've created a story. And without lying. I'm sure the Commendatore will be pleased with you—I mean, with all of us."

"A serious newspaper has to keep files," Lucidi said.

"In what sense?" asked Simei.

"Like pre-obituaries. A newspaper must never find itself unprepared when news of a major death arrives at ten at night and no one's around to piece together a proper obituary in half an hour. That's why most obituaries are written in advance—pre-obits—so when someone dies without warning, you have a ready-made obituary and all you have to do is bring it up to date."

"But our dummy issues aren't being produced one day for the next," I pointed out. "If we are working on one for such-and-such a date, all we have to do is look at the newspapers for that day and we've got our pre-obit."

"Even then, we'll only run it if, let's say, it's the death of a government minister or a big industrialist," explained Simei, "and not some minor poetaster our readers have never heard of. Their only purpose is to take up space in culture sections that major newspapers fill each day with worthless news and comment."

"Pre-obits were just an example," said Lucidi, "but files are important for background information on a particular person in articles of all kinds. They save us last-minute research."

"I understand," said Simei, "but these are luxuries only large newspapers can afford. Keeping files involves tons of research, and I can't let any of you spend all day doing research."

"But you don't have to," Lucidi said, smiling. "All you

need is a student, you pay him a few lire to go around to the newspaper libraries. Don't think files contain anything new, anything that hasn't already been published, and I'm not just talking about newspapers but the secret services as well. Not even the secret services can afford to waste time that way. A file contains press clippings, newspaper articles that say what everyone knows—everyone, that is, except for the minister or opposition leader for whom it's intended, who's never had time to read the newspapers and treats these things like state secrets. Files contain pieces of information that have to be recycled so that suspicions and innuendoes surface. One clipping says so-and-so was fined years ago for speeding, another that last month he visited a Boy Scout camp, and yet another that he was spotted the previous night in a discotheque. From there, you can easily go on to imply that this is someone who recklessly flouts the traffic laws to get to places where alcohol is consumed, and that he probably—I say probably, though it's perfectly apparent—likes young boys. Enough to discredit him, all done by sticking to the simple truth. What's more, the advantage of a file is that it doesn't have to be seen: it's enough for people to know it exists, and that it contains, let us say, interesting information. So-and-so learns that you have information on him, he doesn't know what information, but everyone has some skeleton in the closet, and he is caught in a trap: the minute you put a question to him, he'll see reason."

"I like this idea of files," observed Simei. "Our proprietor would be pleased to have ways of keeping tabs on people who don't much like him, or on those he doesn't much like. Colonna, be so kind as to compile a list of people with whom our proprietor might have dealings, find a hard-up perpetual student, and get him to prepare a dozen or so files. That should do for the moment. An excellent idea, and cheap at the price."

"That's how it's done in politics," concluded Lucidi with a knowing air.

"And you needn't look quite so shocked, Signorina Fresia," snorted Simei. "You mean to say your gossip magazines didn't have their own files? Maybe they sent you off to photograph a pair of actors, or a TV showgirl and a footballer, who'd agreed to pose hand in hand, but to get them there without complaint, your editor would have told them that he would hold back more intimate revelations: perhaps the girl had been caught years earlier in a high-class brothel."

On seeing Maia's face, Lucidi decided to change the subject—perhaps he had a heart after all.

"I've brought other news today, from my own files, of course. On June 5, 1990, Marchese Alessandro Gerini leaves a large fortune to the Fondazione Gerini, an ecclesiastical body under the control of the Salesian Congregation. To this day, no one knows what happened to the money. Some suggest the Salesians received it but are keeping it under wraps for tax reasons. Most likely they haven't yet received it, and it's rumored that the transfer is being handled by a mysterious mediator, perhaps a lawyer, who's claiming a commission that looks very much like a bribe. But other rumors suggest this operation is also being helped along by certain sections of the Salesian Society, so that we're up against an illegal share-out of the cash. For the moment they're only rumors, but I could try to get someone else to talk."

"Try, by all means try," said Simei, "but don't create any bad feeling with the Salesians and the Vatican. Perhaps we could run the headline "Salesians Victims of Fraud?"—with a question mark. That way, we won't cause any problems."

"And if we put 'Salesians in the Eye of the Storm'?" asked Cambria, inept as usual.

"I thought I'd made myself clear," I butted in. "For our readers, 'in the eye of the storm' means someone is in trouble, and some also bring trouble on themselves."

"Right," said Simei. "Let's just stick to spreading suspicion. Someone is involved in fishy business, and though we don't know who it is, we can give him a scare. That's enough for our purposes. Then we'll cash in, or our proprietor can cash in, when the time is right. Well done, Lucidi, carry on. Maximum respect for the Salesians, don't forget, but let them get a little worried, won't do any harm."

"Excuse me," asked Maia timidly, "but does our proprietor . . . or will he be approving this policy, if we can call it that, of files and innuendo? Just so we understand each other."

"We're not accountable to the proprietor for any of our journalistic policies," Simei replied scornfully. "The Commendatore has never sought to influence me in any way. So to work, to work!"

That day I also had a private meeting with Simei. I certainly hadn't forgotten why I was there, and had already sketched out the general outline of several chapters of the book *Domani: Yesterday.* I described more or less the editorial meetings that had taken place, but reversing the roles—in other words, showing Simei as someone who was ready to stand firm against all censure even when his assistants were urging caution. I thought of adding a final chapter in which he received a mellifluous telephone call from a senior prelate close to the Salesians, advising him not to worry himself about the wretched business of Marchese Gerini. Not to mention other telephone calls warning him amicably that it wasn't a good idea to sling mud at the Pio Albergo Trivulzio. But Simei had given a Humphrey Bogart: "It's the press, baby, and there's nothing you can do about it!"

"Magnificent," commented Simei with great excitement. "You're a fine man to work with, Colonna. Let's continue in this vein."

Naturally, I felt more humiliated than Maia with her horoscopes, and for the time being, though the chips were down, I had to carry on playing. Also keeping the South Seas well in sight, wherever they were. Or even just the Ligurian coast—which might be more than enough for a loser.

12

Monday, May 11

Simei called us together the following Monday: "Costanza, in your article about hookers you use such expressions as 'cock-up,' 'crap,' and 'hot shit,' and describe a scene with a hooker who says 'fuck off.'"

"But that's how it is," protested Costanza. "Everyone swears now, on television too, and even ladies say 'fuck.'"

"We're not interested in what they do in high society. We have to think about readers still upset by swear words. You have to use circumlocutions. Colonna?"

I intervened: "One can perfectly well say 'mishap,' 'garbage,' 'bees' knees,' and 'take a running jump.'"

"Breaking a leg in the process," sneered Braggadocio.

"Whether they break a leg is none of our business," replied Simei.

Then we turned to other matters. An hour later, when the meeting was over, Maia took me and Braggadocio aside:

"I don't take part any longer, since I'm always wrong, but it would be nice to publish an alternative handbook."

"Alternative to what?" asked Braggadocio.

"To the swear words we were talking about."

"That was an hour ago!" exclaimed Braggadocio, eyeing me as if to say, You see, she's always doing it.

"Ignore it," I told him in a conciliatory tone, "if she's still thinking about it . . . So, Maia, let's hear your innermost thoughts."

"Well, it would be nice, instead of saying 'fuck' each time, to express surprise or consternation by saying 'Oh, coitus, I've had my purse stolen!'"

"She's crazy," Braggadocio whispered in my ear. "Colonna, could you come to my desk? I have something to show you."

I went off with him, winking at Maia, whose autism, if that's what it was, I was finding more and more delightful.

Everyone had left the office, it was getting dark, and under the light of a desk lamp Braggadocio laid out a set of photocopies.

"Colonna," he began, spreading his arms around the papers before him as though he didn't want anyone to see them, "look at these documents, I found them in the archives. The day after Mussolini's corpse had been displayed in Piazzale Loreto, it was taken to the Institute of Forensic Medicine at the university for the autopsy, and here's the doctor's report:

"'Istituto di Medicina Legale e delle Assicurazioni della Regia Università di Milano, Professor Mario Cattabeni, Autopsy

Report No. 7241, performed April 30, 1945, on the corpse of Benito Mussolini, deceased April 28, 1945. Body prepared on the anatomy table unclothed. Weight, seventy-two kilograms. Height, one point sixty-six meters, measured approximately due to the conspicuous traumatic transformation of head. Face disfigured by multiple gunshot wounds and contusions rendering facial features almost unrecognizable. Anthropometric measurements of head not carried out because deformed by fracture inflicted on craniofacial skeleton . . .' Let's move on: 'Head, deformed by complete skeletal collapse, with deep depression of entire left parietal-occipital region and crushing of orbital region of same side, where eyeball appears deflated and torn with complete discharge of vitreous humor; adipose tissue of eye socket extensively exposed by wide laceration, not infiltrated with blood. In median frontal region and left parietal-frontal area, two extensive continual linear gashes to scalp, with lacerated edges, each around six centimeters wide, exposing cranium. In occipital region to right of median line, two holes close together with everted, irregular edges of around two centimeters maximum diameter out of which emerges brain matter reduced to pulp with no appearance of hematic infiltration.' You understand? Brain reduced to a pulp!"

Braggadocio was almost sweating, his hands shook, his lower lip beaded with drops of saliva, he had the expression of an excited glutton sniffing fried brains, a succulent plate of tripe, or a goulash. And he continued.

"'At back of neck, short distance from right of median

line, wide lacerated hole of almost three centimeters diameter with everted edges, not infiltrated with blood. In right temporal region, two holes close together, roundish, edges finely lacerated, not infiltrated with blood. In left temporal region, wide lacerated opening with everted edges and emergence of brain matter reduced to pulp. Vast exit hole at base of left earlobe: last two lesions have typical appearance of postmortem injuries. At base of nose, small lacerated hole with everted comminuted bone fragments, moderately infiltrated with blood. To right cheek, group of three holes followed by direct deep passage backward, with slight backward skew, with funnel-shaped inward edges, not infiltrated with blood. Comminuted fracture of upper jaw with extensive laceration of soft and skeletal parts of palatal arch having nature of postmortem injury.' I'll jump forward again, as they're observations on the position of injuries and we're not interested how and where he was struck, all we need to know is that they shot him. 'Comminuted fracture to skull bounded by numerous mobile fragments removed offering direct access to endocranial cavity. Thickness of skull bone normal. Pachymeninx deflated with large tears in anterior half: no trace of epi- or hypodural hemorrhagic effusion. Removal of brain cannot be fully performed, as cerebellum, pons, mesencephalon, and a lower portion of cerebral lobes appear reduced to pulp.'"

He emphasized the word "pulp" each time, which Professor Cattabeni used excessively—no doubt impressed by how the corpse had been battered—and he pronounced it with a kind of sensual pleasure, roundly enunciating each *p*. It reminded me of Dario Fo's *Mistero Buffo,* Fo himself in the role of a peasant gorging himself on a dish he has always dreamed of.

"Let's move on. 'The only intact parts are most of hemispherical convexities, corpus callosum, and part of base of brain. Arteries of encephalic base are only partly identifiable among mobile fragments of comminuted fracture of entire cranial base and still partly connected to encephalic mass: trunks thus identified, including anterior cerebral arteries, appear as healthy walls . . .' And do you think a doctor, who in any event was convinced he had the body of the Duce in front of him, was capable of figuring out who that mass of flesh and shattered bones really belonged to? And work peacefully in a room where, and it is a matter of record, people were wandering in and out—journalists, partisans, curious onlookers? And where intestines lay abandoned on the corner of a table, and two nurses played Ping-Pong with the offal, throwing pieces of liver or lung at each other?"

As he talked, Braggadocio looked like a cat who had sneakily jumped on a butcher's counter. If he'd had whiskers, they would have bristled and quivered.

"And if you go on reading, you'll see there was no trace of an ulcer in the stomach, and we all know that Mussolini had one, nor is there mention of traces of syphilis, and yet it was common knowledge that the deceased was in an advanced stage of syphilis. Note also that Georg Zachariae, a German doctor who had treated the Duce at Salò, had stated shortly afterward that his patient suffered from low blood pressure, anemia, enlarged liver, stomach cramps, twisted bowel, and acute constipation. And yet, according to the autopsy, everything was normal: liver of regular size and appearance both externally and upon incision, bile ducts healthy, renal and suprarenal glands intact, urinary tract and genitals normal. Final note: 'Brain, removed in residual parts, was fixed in liquid formalin for later anatomical and histopathological examination, fragment of cortex given on request by Health Office of Fifth Army Command (Calvin S. Drayer) to Dr. Winfred H. Overholser of Saint Elizabeths Psychiatric Hospital in Washington.' Over and out."

He read and savored each line as if he were in front of the corpse, as if touching it, as if he were at Taverna Moriggi and, instead of shank of pork with sauerkraut, he was slavering over that orbital region where the eyeball appeared deflated and torn with complete discharge of the vitreous humor, as if he were savoring the pons, the mesencephalus, the lower part of the cerebral lobes, as if he were exulting over the emergence of the almost liquefied brain matter.

I was disgusted, but—I cannot deny it—fascinated by him and by the martyred corpse over which he exulted, in the same way readers of nineteenth-century novels were hypnotized by the gaze of the serpent. To put an end to his exultation, I said, "It's the autopsy on . . . well, it could be anyone."

"Exactly. You see, my theory was correct: Mussolini's corpse wasn't that of Mussolini, and in any case, no one could swear it was his. I'm now reasonably clear about what happened between April 25 and 30."

That evening I really felt the need to cleanse myself, be with Maia. And to distance her in my mind from the other members of the team, I decided to tell her the truth, that *Domani* would never be published.

"It's better that way," said Maia. "I won't have to worry about the future. We'll hold out for a few months, earn ourselves those few lire—few, filthy, and fast—and then the South Seas."

13

Late May

My life was now running along parallel lines. By day the humiliating existence at the newspaper, in the evening Maia's little apartment, also mine sometimes. Saturdays and Sundays to Lake Orta. The evenings compensated us both for days spent with Simei. Maia had given up making suggestions that would only be rejected, and confined herself to sharing them with me, for amusement, or for consolation.

One evening she showed me a lonelyhearts magazine. "Great," she said, "except that I'd love to try publishing them with the subtext."

"In what way?"

"This way: 'Hi, I'm Samantha, twenty-nine years old, professionally qualified, housewife, separated, no children, seeking a man, attractive, bright, and sociable.' Subtext: I'm now thirty. After my husband left, I had no luck finding a job with the bookkeeping diploma I worked hard to get. I am stuck at home all day twiddling my thumbs. (I don't even have any brats to look after.) I'm looking for a man, he doesn't have to be handsome, provided he doesn't knock me around like that bastard I married.

"Or: 'Carolina, age thirty-three, unmarried, graduate, businesswoman, sophisticated, dark hair, slim, confident and sincere, interested in sports, movies, theater, travel, reading, dancing, open to new experiences, would like to meet interesting man with personality, education and good position, professional, executive or military, max. sixty years with view to marriage.' Subtext: At thirty-three I'm still on the shelf, perhaps because I'm skinny as a rake and would like to be blond but try not to worry about it. I struggled to get an arts degree but couldn't get a job with it, so I set up a small workshop where I employ three Albanians, paid in cash; we produce socks for the local market stalls. I don't really know what I like, I watch some television, go to the movies with a friend or to the local amateur dramatic society, I read the newspaper, especially the lonelyhearts pages, I like dancing but don't have anyone to take me, and to land a husband I'm prepared to take an interest in anything, so long as there's money so I can ditch the socks and the Albanians. I don't mind if he's old, an accountant if possible, but I'd also settle for a registry clerk or a retired policeman.

"Or this one: 'Patrizia, age forty-two, single, shopkeeper, dark, slender, sweet and sensitive, would like to meet a man who is loyal, kind and sincere, marital status unimportant so long as he's motivated.' Subtext: Hell, at forty-two (and with a name like Patrizia I must be going on fifty, like every other Patrizia), not married, I make ends meet with the haberdashery shop my poor mother left me. I am slightly anorexic and basically neurotic; is there a man out there who will take me to bed? Doesn't matter whether he's married or not, so long as he fucks well.

"And again: 'Still hoping there's a woman capable of true love. I'm a bachelor, bank clerk, age twenty-nine, reasonably good-looking and a lively character, seeking a pretty girl, serious, educated, able to sweep me off my feet.' Subtext: I don't really get along with women, the few I've met were morons, all they wanted was to get married. They say I have a lively character because I tell them exactly where to get off. I'm not a complete jerk, so isn't there some sex bomb who doesn't pop her gum and say 'dese' and 'dose,' who's up for a good fuck without expecting too much else?"

"You don't seriously want Simei to publish stuff like that. Or rather, the announcements might be okay, but not your interpretations!"

"I know, I know," said Maia, "but there's nothing wrong with dreaming."

Then, as we were falling asleep, she said, "You who know everything, do you know why they say 'Lose Trebizond and clash the cymbals'?"

"No, I don't, but is this the kind of question to ask at midnight?"

"Well, I actually do know. There are two explanations. One is that since Trebizond was the main port on the Black Sea, if trading ships lost their way to Trebizond, it meant losing the money invested in the voyage. The other, which seems more likely, is that Trebizond was the navigation point ships looked for, and losing sight of it meant losing direction, or your bearings, or where you're going. As for 'clash the cymbals,' which is commonly used to mean a state of drunkenness, the etymological dictionary tells us that it originally meant being excessively lively, was used by Pietro Aretino, and comes from Psalm 150, *Laudate eum in cymbalis bene sonantibus*, 'Praise him with the clash of cymbals.'"

"Look who I've ended up with. You're so curious, how did you deal for so long with celebrity romances?"

"For money, filthy lucre. It happens when you're a loser." She held me closer. "But I'm less of a loser now that I've won you in the lottery."

What do you do with a screwball like that, other than go back to making love? And in doing so, I felt almost a winner.

We hadn't been watching television on the evening of the twenty-third, so it was only the following day that we read in the papers about the killing of the anti-Mafia judge Giovanni Falcone. We were shocked and, next morning at the office, also visibly upset.

Costanza asked Simei whether we shouldn't do an issue on the assassination. "Let's think about it," said Simei doubtfully. "If we talk about the death of Falcone, we have to talk about the Mafia, complain about the lack of policing, things like that. Right away we make enemies with the police and with the Cosa Nostra. I don't know whether the Commendatore would like that. When we start a real newspaper, and a magistrate is blown up, then we'll certainly have to comment on it, and in commenting on it we're immediately in danger of putting forward ideas that will be contradicted a few days later. That's a risk a real newspaper has to run, but why us now? The wiser course, even for a real newspaper, is generally to keep it sentimental, to interview the relatives. If you watch carefully, that's what they do on TV when they go doorstepping the mother whose ten-year-old son has been killed in a tank of acid: How do you feel, signora, about your son's death? People shed a few tears and everyone's happy. Like that lovely German word *Schadenfreude,* pleasure at other people's misfortune, a sentiment that a newspaper has to respect and nurture. But for the moment we don't have to concern ourselves with these miseries, and indignation should be left to left-wing newspapers, that's their specialty. Besides, it's not such incredible news. Magistrates have been killed before, and they'll be killed again. We'll have plenty of good opportunities. For the moment let's hold back."

Falcone having been eliminated twice over, we turned to more serious matters.

Braggadocio came up to me, gave me a nudge: "See? This whole business confirms my story."

"What the hell has it got to do with your story?"

"I don't know yet, but it's got to have something to do with it. Everything always fits with everything else, you just have to know how to read the coffee grounds. Give me time."

14

Wednesday, May 27

ONE MORNING, AS SHE WOKE UP, Maia said, "But I don't much like him."

By now I was ready for her synaptic games.

"You're talking about Braggadocio," I said.

"Of course, who else?" Then, almost as an afterthought, "How did you figure that out?"

"*My dear,* as Simei would say, the two of us know a total of six people in common. I thought of the one who'd been the rudest to you and hit on Braggadocio."

"I could have been thinking about, I don't know, President Cossiga."

"But you weren't, you were thinking of Braggadocio. And anyway, for once I've caught your train of thought, so why do you want to complicate matters?"

"See how you're beginning to think what I think?"

And, damn it, she was right.

• • •

"Queers," announced Simei that morning at the daily editorial meeting. "Queers are a subject that always attracts attention."

"You don't say 'queer' anymore," ventured Maia. "You say 'gay,' no?"

"I know, my dear, I know." Simei was irritated. "But our readers still say 'queer,' or rather, they think it, since it disgusts them even to say it. I know you don't say 'Negro' any longer but 'black.' You don't say 'blind' but 'visually impaired.' But a black is still black, and a visually impaired person can't see a lucifer, poor thing. I've nothing against queers, same as Negroes, for me they are absolutely fine so long as they mind their own business."

"So why write about gays if our readers find them disgusting?"

"I'm not thinking about queers in general, my dear, I'm all for freedom, everyone can do as they please. But some of them are in politics, in parliament, and in government. People think queers are just writers and ballet dancers, yet some are in positions of power and we don't even know it. They're a Mafia, helping each other out. And this is something our readers might like to know."

Maia wasn't prepared to give in: "But things are changing, maybe in ten years a gay will be able to say he's gay without anyone batting an eyelid."

"All sorts of things can happen in ten years, we're all aware that morals are declining. But for the moment this is a matter of concern to our readers. Lucidi, you've plenty of sources, give us something on queers in politics—but be careful, don't name names, we don't want to end up in court, we just want to float the idea, the specter, create a shiver, a sense of unease . . ."

"I can give you plenty of names if you wish," said Lucidi. "But if, as you say, it's just a matter of creating unease, according to what I've heard, there's a bookshop in Rome where high-ranking homosexuals meet unnoticed, the place is mostly visited by normal people. And for some it's also a place where they can get a bindle of cocaine. You pick up a book, take it to the counter, and the assistant will slip in the bindle along with the book. It's well known that . . . well, mentioning no names, one was also a minister, and a homosexual, and he is given to snorting coke. Everyone knows, or anyone of any importance. It's not a place for your garden-variety butt boy, nor the ballet dancer who'd camp around and attract too much attention."

"It's fine to talk about rumors, with a few spicy details, just a bit of color. But there's also a way of introducing names. You can say that the place is totally respectable since it's frequented by eminent personalities, and there you can throw in seven or eight names of writers, journalists, and senators of impeccable character. Except that among these names you include one or two queers. No one can say we are libeling anyone, because those names appear as examples of people of integrity. Indeed, we can include a card-carrying womanizer whose lover's name we know. Meanwhile we've sent out a coded message for those ready to listen, and someone will have understood that we could say much more if we wanted."

Maia was shocked. She left before the others, motioning

to me as if to say, Sorry, I have to be alone tonight, I'm taking a sleeping pill and going straight to bed. And so I fell prey to Braggadocio, who continued regaling me with his stories as we strolled off and, by pure coincidence, ended up in Via Bagnera, as if the somber air of the place suited the morbid nature of his tale.

"So, listen, here I seem to be running up against a series of events that go against my theory, though you'll see it's not quite like that. Anyway, Mussolini, now reduced to offal, is stitched more or less back together, and buried with Claretta and the rest of them in the main Musocco cemetery, but in an unmarked tomb so no one could turn it into a place of Fascist pilgrimage. This must have been the wish of whoever had let the real Mussolini escape, to minimize talk of his death. They certainly couldn't create the myth of Barbarossa hidden away in a cave, which might work well for Hitler since no one knew what had happened to his body or whether he had actually died. But while letting it be thought that Mussolini was dead (and partisans continued to celebrate Piazzale Loreto as one of the magical moments of the liberation), they had to be prepared for the idea that one day the deceased would resurface—as new, as good as new, as the song goes. And there's no way of resurrecting anything from patched-up pulp. But at this point that spoilsport Domenico Leccisi appears on the scene."

"He was the one who snatched the Duce's corpse, wasn't he?"

"Exactly. A twenty-six-year-old goon, the last firebrand of Salò, full of ideals but no ideas. He wants to give his idol a decent burial, or at least create a scandal to publicize the resurgence of neofascism, and he puts together a band of crazies like himself to go to the cemetery one night in April 1946. The few watchmen are fast asleep. He goes straight to the grave, obviously he has inside information. He digs up the body, now in a worse state than when it was boxed up—after all, a year had gone by, and I'll let you picture what he must have found—and pitter-patter hush-hush he carries it away as best he can, leaving a scrap of decomposed tissue and even two bones lying along the cemetery path. I mean to say, what idiocy."

I had the impression Braggadocio would have truly enjoyed being involved in that macabre transportation: his necrophilia had prepared me for anything.

"Shock, horror, newspaper headlines," he went on, "police searching everywhere for a hundred days, unable to trace the fetid remains, despite the trail of stench that must have been left along the route they'd taken. But the first of the accomplices, Mauro Rana, is caught after just a few days, and then the others, one by one, until Leccisi himself is arrested in late July. And it's determined that the corpse had been hidden for a short while at Rana's house in the Valtellina, then, in May, handed over to Father Zucca, the Franciscan prior of the Convent of Sant'Angelo in Milan, who had walled it up in the right-hand nave of his church. The problem of Father Zucca and his assistant, Father Parini, is quite another story. There are those who saw them as chaplains to a high-society and reactionary Milan, involved with neofascist circles in trafficking forged banknotes and drugs, while for others they were goodhearted friars who couldn't refuse to perform what was the duty of every good Christian—*parce sepulto,* to spare the corpse. I have very little interest in all this, but what does interest me is that the government, with the agreement of Cardinal Schuster, orders the body to be interred in the Capuchin convent of Cerro Maggiore, and there it remains, from 1946 to 1957, eleven years, without the secret ever getting out. You must realize that this is a crucial part of the story. That idiot Leccisi had risked dragging out the corpse of Mussolini's double, not that it could have been examined in that state, yet for those pulling the strings in the Mussolini affair, it was better to keep things hushed up, the less said the better. But while Leccisi (after twenty-one months' imprisonment) sets out on a glorious parliamentary career, the new prime minister, Adone Zoli, who had managed to form a government thanks to the votes of the neofascists, agrees in exchange to allow the body to be returned to the family, and it is interred in Mussolini's hometown of Predappio, in a shrine that even today is a rallying point for diehard old Fascists and young fanatics, black shirts and Roman salutes. I don't think Zoli knew anything about the existence of the real Mussolini, so he wasn't worried about the cult of the double. It may have happened differently, I don't know. Perhaps the business of the double was being handled not by the neofascists but by others much higher up."

"Wait, what's the role of Mussolini's family in all this? Either they don't know the Duce's alive, which seems impossible, or they agreed to bring home a bogus corpse."

"You know, I still haven't worked out the family situation. I think they knew their husband and father was alive somewhere. If he'd been hidden away in the Vatican, it would have been hard to visit him—none of the family could walk into the Vatican without being noticed. Argentina is the better bet. The evidence? Take Vittorio Mussolini. He escapes the purges, becomes a scriptwriter, and lives in Argentina for a long period after the war. In Argentina, you understand? To be near his father? We can't be sure, but why Argentina? And there are photos of Romano Mussolini and other people at Ciampino Airport in Rome saying goodbye to Vittorio on his departure for Buenos Aires. Why give so much importance to the journey of a brother who before the war had already been traveling as far as the United States? And Romano? After the war he makes a name for himself as a jazz pianist, also playing abroad. History certainly hasn't concerned itself about Romano's concert tours, and who knows whether he too had been to Argentina? And Mussolini's wife? She was free to move around, nobody would have stopped her taking a holiday, perhaps in Paris or Geneva so as not to draw attention, and from there to Buenos Aires. Who knows? When Leccisi and Zoli create the mess we've seen and suddenly bring out what's left of the corpse, she could hardly say it belonged to someone else. She makes the best of a bad job and puts it in the family vault—it serves to keep the Fascist spirit alive among the old guard while she waits for the real Duce to come back. But I'm not interested in the family story; this is where the second part of my investigation begins."

"So what happens next?"

"It's past dinnertime, and a few pieces of my mosaic are still missing. We'll talk about it next time."

I couldn't figure out whether Braggadocio was a brilliant narrator who was feeding me his story in installments, with the necessary suspense at each "to be continued," or whether he was still actually trying to piece the plot together. I preferred not to insist, however, for in the meantime all the comings and goings of malodorous remains had turned my stomach. I went home.

15

Thursday, May 28

"For issue number 0/2," Simei announced that morning, "we need to think of an article about honesty. It's a fact, now, that the political parties are rotten, everyone's after kickbacks, and we have to make it known that we're in a position, if we so wish, to initiate a campaign against those parties. We have to come up with a party of honest people, a party of citizens able to talk a different kind of politics."

"We'd better tread carefully," I said. "Wasn't that the idea behind the postwar movement that called itself the Common Man?"

"Ah, the Common Man, that was swallowed up and emasculated by the Christian Democratic Party, which at that time was powerful and extremely cunning. But the Christian Democrats today are on their last legs—no more heroes, they're a bunch of jerks. In any event, our readers don't remember a thing about the Common Man," said Simei. "It's the stuff of forty-five years ago, and our readers don't have a clue what happened ten years ago. I've just been reading an article celebrating the Resistance in one of the main newspapers, and there are two photographs, one of a truckload of partisans and the other of a group wearing Fascist uniforms and giving the Roman salute, who are described as *squadristi*. But no, *squadristi* were the squads of the 1920s, and they didn't go around dressed like that; those in the photo are Fascist troops of the '30s or early '40s, as anyone my age would instantly recognize. I'm not suggesting all journalists have to be people my age who have witnessed such events, but I'm perfectly capable of distinguishing the uniforms of the *bersaglieri* of La Marmora from the troops of Bava-Beccaris, though both of them died out well before I was born. If our newspaper colleagues have such poor memories, then why count on our readers to remember the Common Man? But let's go back to my idea: a new party, a party of honest people could trouble a great many."

"*League of the Honest,*" said Maia with a smile. "That was the title of an old prewar novel by Giovanni Mosca. It would be interesting to reread it. It's about the *union sacrée* of decent people whose task it was to infiltrate the ranks of the dishonest, expose them, and convert them if possible to the path of honesty. But to be accepted by dishonest people, members of the league had to behave dishonestly. You can imagine what happened. The league of honest people gradually turned into a league of crooks."

"That's literature, my dear," snapped Simei, "and Mosca, does anyone still remember him? You read too much. We can forget your Mosca, but if the idea appalls you, you don't need to worry about it. Dottor Colonna, you'll give me a hand to write a lead article that's hard-hitting. And virtuous."

"Can do," I said. "Appealing to honest folk is always excellent for sales."

"The league of honest crooks," sneered Braggadocio, looking at Maia. The two of them were not made for each other. I felt increasingly sorry for this little walking encyclopedia who was a prisoner in Simei's den. But I could see no way to help her right now. Her problem was becoming my chief concern (maybe hers too?), and I was losing interest in the rest.

At lunchtime, walking to a bar for a sandwich, I said to her, "Do you want us to put a stop to it? Why not expose this whole pathetic story, and to hell with Simei and company?"

"And who do we go to?" she asked. "First of all, don't destroy yourself on my account. Second, where do you go to expose this business when every newspaper . . . I'm just beginning to understand, aren't they all exactly the same? Each protects the other . . ."

"Now don't get like Braggadocio, who sees plots everywhere. Anyway, forgive me, I'm just talking . . ." I didn't know how to say it. "I think I love you."

"Do you realize that's the first time you've told me?"

"Stupid, don't we think the same way?"

It was true. At least thirty years had gone by since I'd said anything like that. It was May, and after thirty years I was feeling spring in my bones.

• • •

Why did I think of bones? It was that same afternoon that Braggadocio told me to meet him in the Verziere district, in front of the Church of San Bernardino alle Ossa, which stood along a passageway at the corner of Piazza Santo Stefano.

"Nice church," said Braggadocio as we entered. "It's been here since the Middle Ages, but after destruction, fire, and other mishaps, it wasn't until the 1700s that it was rebuilt. The original purpose was to house the bones of a leper cemetery not far from here."

I should have guessed. Having told me about Mussolini's corpse, which he could hardly dig up again, Braggadocio was seeking other mortuary inspirations. And indeed, along a corridor, we entered the ossuary. The place was deserted, except for an old woman praying in a front pew with her head between her hands. There were death's heads crammed into high recesses between one pilaster and another, boxes of bones, skulls arranged in the shape of a cross set into a mosaic of whitish stone-like objects that were other bones, perhaps fragments of vertebrae, limb joints, collarbones, breastbones, shoulder blades, coccyges, carpals and metacarpals, kneecaps, etarsal and ankle bones, and suchlike. Bone edifices rose on every side, leading the eye up to a merry, luminous Tiepolesque vault, where angels and souls in glory hovered among billowing, creamy pink clouds.

On a shelf over an old door were skulls with gaping eye sockets, lined up like porcelain jars in a pharmacist's cabinet. In the recesses at floor level, protected by a grill through which visitors could poke their fingers, the bones and skulls had been polished and smoothed over many centuries from the touch of devotees or necrophiles, like the foot of Saint Peter's statue in Rome. There were at least a thousand skulls, the smaller bones were beyond count, and on the pilasters were monograms of Christ, along with tibias that looked like they'd been stolen from the Jolly Rogers of the pirates of Tortuga.

"They're not just the bones of lepers," explained Braggadocio, as though nothing in the world could be more beautiful. "There are skeletons from other nearby burial grounds, the corpses of convicts, deceased patients from the Brolo hospital, beheaded criminals, prisoners who died in jail, probably also thieves or brigands who came to die in the church because there was no place else they could turn their face to the wall in peace—the Verziere was a district with a terrible reputation. It makes me laugh to see that old woman sitting here praying as if before the tomb of a saint with holy relics, when these are the remains of scoundrels, bandits, damned souls. And yet the old monks were more compassionate than those who buried and then dug up Mussolini. See with what care, with what devotion to art—and yet with what indifference—these skeletal remains were arranged, as if they were Byzantine mosaics. That little old woman is seduced by these images of death, mistaking them for images of sanctity, and yet under the altar, though I can no longer see where, you should be able to see the half-mummified body of a young girl who, they say, comes out on the Night of All Souls to perform her *danse macabre* with the other skeletons."

I pictured the young girl leading her bony friends as far as Via Bagnera, but made no comment. I had seen other, equally macabre ossuaries, like the one in the Capuchin church in

Rome, and the terrifying catacombs in Palermo, with whole mummified friars dressed in tattered majesty, but Braggadocio was evidently quite content with his Milanese carcasses.

"There's also the putridarium, which you reach by going down some steps in front of the main altar, but you have to search out the sacristan, and you need to find him in a good mood. The friars used to place their brothers on stone seats to decay and dissolve, and slowly the bodies dehydrated, the humors drained away. And here are the skeletons, picked clean as the teeth in toothpaste ads. A few days ago I was thinking this would have been an ideal place to hide Mussolini's corpse after Leccisi had stolen it, but unfortunately I'm not writing a novel but reconstructing historical facts, and history tells us the remains of the Duce were placed somewhere else. Shame. That's why recently I've been visiting this place a lot, for a story about last remains. It's been giving me much food for thought. There are those who find inspiration looking, say, at the Dolomites or Lake Maggiore, but I find inspiration here. I should have been the keeper of a morgue. Perhaps it's the memory of my grandfather who died so horribly, may he rest in peace."

"Why have you brought *me* here?"

"I need to talk, I've got to tell someone about these things seething inside me, or else I'll go mad. It can turn your head being the only person to have found the truth. And there's never anyone here, except for the occasional tourist, who doesn't understand a damn thing. And at last I've reached stay-behind."

"Stay *what?*"

"Remember I still had to work out what they did with the Duce, the living one—not to leave him rotting in Argentina or in the Vatican and ending up like his double. What do we do with the Duce?"

"What *do* we do with him?"

"Well, the Allies, or those among the Allies who wanted him alive, to be brought out at the right moment, to be used against a Communist revolution or a Soviet attack. During the Second World War, the British had coordinated the activities of the resistance movements in the countries occupied by the Axis powers through a network run by a branch of their intelligence services, the Special Operations Executive, which was disbanded at the end of the war. But it was started up again in the early 1950s as the nucleus for a new organization that was to operate in various European countries to stop an invasion by the Red Army, or local Communists who might try to overthrow the state. The coordination was done by the supreme command of the Allied forces in Europe, and led to the creation of 'stay-behind' in Belgium, England, France, West Germany, Holland, Luxembourg, Denmark, and Norway. A secret paramilitary structure. In Italy, its beginnings can be traced back to 1949; then, in 1959, the Italian secret services enter as part of a coordination and planning committee, and finally in 1964 the organization called Gladio was officially born, funded by the CIA. Gladio—the word ought to mean something to you, since *gladius* was a sword used by Roman legionaries, so using the word *gladio* evoked the imagery of fascism. A name that would attract military veterans, adventurers, and nostalgics. The war was over, but many people had fond memories of heroic days, of attacks with a couple of bombs and a flower in their mouth (as the Fascist song went), of machine-gun fire. They were ex-Fascists, or idealistic sixty-year-old Catholics terrified at the prospect of Cossacks arriving at Saint Peter's and letting their horses drink from the holy-water stoups, but there were also fanatics loyal to the exiled monarchy. It's even rumored that they included Edgardo Sogno, who, though once a partisan leader in Piedmont and a hero, was also a monarchist through and through, and therefore linked to the creed of a bygone world. Recruits were sent to a training camp in Sardinia, where they learned (or were reminded) how to blow up bridges, operate machine guns, attack enemy squads at night with daggers between their teeth, carry out acts of sabotage and guerrilla warfare—"

"But they would all have been retired colonels, ailing field marshals, rachitic bank clerks. I can't see them clambering over piers and pylons like in *The Bridge over the River Kwai*."

"Yes, but there were also young neofascists raring for a fight, and all kinds of angry types who had nothing to do with politics."

"I seem to remember reading something about it a few years ago."

"Certainly, Gladio remained top secret from the end of the war, the only people to know about it were the intelligence services and the highest military commanders, and it was communicated little by little only to prime ministers, ministers of defense, and presidents of the republic. With the collapse of the Soviet empire, the whole thing lost all practical purpose, and perhaps cost too much. It was President

Cossiga who let the cat out of the bag in 1990, and then, the same year, Prime Minister Andreotti officially admitted that, all right, Gladio had existed, but there was no reason to fuss, its existence had been necessary, the story was now over, and the tittle-tattle was to stop. As it turned out, no one was overconcerned, the issue was almost forgotten. Italy, Belgium, and Switzerland were the only countries to launch parliamentary inquiries, but George H. W. Bush refused to comment since he was in the midst of preparations for the Gulf War and didn't want to unsettle the Atlantic Alliance. The entire affair was hushed up in all the countries that participated in the stay-behind operations, with only a few minor incidents. In France it had been known for some time that the infamous OAS had been created with members of the French stay-behind, but after a failed coup in Algiers, General de Gaulle had brought dissidents back under control. In Germany, it was common knowledge that the Oktoberfest bomb in Munich in 1980 was made with explosives that came from a German stay-behind depot; in Greece, it was the stay-behind army, the Lochos Oreinon Katadromon, that kicked off the military coup, and in Portugal, a mysterious Aginter Press was behind the assassination of Eduardo Mondlane, leader of the Frente de Libertação de Moçambique. In Spain, a year after the death of General Franco, two members of the Carlist Party were killed by far-right terrorists, and the following year, stay-behinds carried out a massacre in Madrid, in the office of a lawyer with links to the Communist Party. In Switzerland, just two years ago, Colonel Alboth, a former local stay-behind commander, declares in a private letter to the Swiss defense department that he is prepared to reveal "the whole truth" and is then found dead at his home, stabbed with his own bayonet. In Turkey, the Grey Wolves, later involved in the assassination attempt on Pope John Paul II, are linked to stay-behind. I could go on—and I've read you only a few of my notes—but as you see, this is small stuff, a killing here and a killing there, barely enough to reach the front page, and each time all is forgotten. The point is that newspapers are not there for spreading news but for covering it up. X happens, you have to report it, but it causes embarrassment for too many people, so in the same edition you add some shock headlines—mother kills four children, savings at risk of going up in smoke, letter from Garibaldi insulting his lieutenant Nino Bixio discovered, etc.—so news drowns in a great sea of information. I'm interested in what Gladio did in Italy from the 1960s until 1990. Must have been up to all kinds of tricks, would have been mixed up with the far-right terrorist movements, played a part in the bombing at Piazza Fontana in 1969, and from then on—the days of the student revolts of '68 and the workers' strikes that autumn—it dawned on someone that he could incite terrorist attacks and put the blame on the Left. And it's rumored that Licio Gelli's notorious P2 Masonic lodge was also sticking its nose in. But why is an organization that should have been opposing the Soviets involving itself in terrorist attacks? And here I came across the whole story of Prince Junio Valerio Borghese, and before that, all those rumors of military takeovers planned but never carried out."

The so-called Borghese coup was a fairly grotesque story

that someone, I think, turned into a satirical movie. Junio Valerio Borghese, also known as the Black Prince, had been a leader of the Decima Mas commando unit. A man of some courage, it was said, a Fascist through and through, he had inevitably been part of Mussolini's Republic of Salò, and it was never clear how, in 1945, while people were being shot at random, he managed to survive, and continued to preserve the aura of a thoroughbred fighter, beret at a rakish angle, machine gun slung across his shoulder, typical military garb with trousers gathered at the ankles, turtleneck sweater, though he had a face that no one would have looked at twice if they'd seen him walking in the street dressed as a bank clerk.

Now, in 1970, Borghese felt the moment for a military coup had come. Mussolini would have been approaching eighty-seven by then. They must have realized, Braggadocio thought, that if he was to be brought back from exile, it was better not to wait too much longer—after all, back in 1945 he was already looking worn.

"My heart sometimes goes out to that poor man," said Braggadocio. "Imagine him still waiting patiently . . . assuming he was in Argentina, where even if he couldn't eat the great beefsteaks because of his ulcer, he could at least look out over the boundless pampas (even so, what bliss—just think—for twenty-five years). It would have been worse if he'd been shut up in the Vatican, with no more than an evening walk in a small garden, and vegetable broth served by a nun with hairs on her chin, and the idea of having lost not only Italy but his lover, unable to hug his children, and perhaps going slightly soft in the head, spending day after day in an armchair brooding over past glories, only able to see what was going on in the world through the television, black and white, while he thought back—his mind now clouding with age but roused by syphilis—to triumphant moments on the balcony of Palazzo Venezia, to summers when he harvested the corn barechested, smothered children with kisses while their aroused mothers slavered over his hands, or the afternoons in the Sala del Mappamondo, where his manservant, Navarra, would bring women in for him and, unbuttoning his fly in cavalry fashion, he would flip them over on his desk and, *wham,* inseminate them in seconds while they made simpering groans like bitches in heat, murmuring, 'Oh, my Duce, my Duce' . . . And as he thought back, salivating, his cock now flaccid, someone was hammering away in his head about the idea of resurrection close at hand—like the joke about Hitler, who's also in Argentina, and the neo-Nazis want him to come back and conquer the world, and he hems and haws, since he too is getting old, and finally he says, 'Okay, but this time as *baddies,* right?'

"Anyhow," continued Braggadocio, "in 1970 everything seemed to suggest a military coup might work. The head of the Italian secret services was General Miceli, who was also a member of the P2 Masonic lodge and would later become a politician and member of the Neofascist Party—note that he was suspected and investigated for involvement in the Borghese affair, though he got through it unscathed and died peacefully two years ago. I've learned from a reliable source that Miceli, two years after the Borghese coup, still received eight hundred thousand dollars from the American embassy, no one knows why. Borghese could therefore rely on excellent support from the top, and on Gladio, on the Falangist veterans of the Spanish Civil War, on Masonic contacts, and it has been implied that the Mafia played a part—which, as you know, it always does. And in the shadows, the ubiquitous Licio Gelli stirring up the police and the top military command, which already swarmed with Freemasons. Just listen to the story of Licio Gelli, because it's central to my theory.

"So Gelli, he's never denied it, fought in the Spanish Civil War with Franco. And he was in the Italian Social Republic and worked as a liaison officer with the SS, but at the same time he had contacts with the partisans, and after the war he links up with the CIA. Someone like that could hardly fail to be mixed up with Gladio. But hear this: in July 1942, as an inspector of the National Fascist Party, he was given the task of transporting the treasury of King Peter II of Yugoslavia into Italy: sixty tons of gold ingots, two tons of old coinage, six million U.S. dollars, and two million pounds sterling that the Military Intelligence Service had requisitioned. The treasury was finally returned in 1947, twenty tons of ingots light, and it is rumored that Gelli had moved them to Argentina. Argentina, you understand? In Argentina, Gelli is on friendly terms with Perón, and not just with Perón but with generals such as Videla, and from Argentina he receives a diplomatic passport. Who else is mixed up with Argentina? His right-hand man, Umberto Ortolani, who is also the link between Gelli and Monsignor Marcinkus. And so? So everything points us to Argentina, where the Duce is living and preparing for his return, and there's obviously a need for money and good organization and local support. Which is why Gelli is essential to the Borghese plan."

"It sounds convincing, doesn't it."

"And it is. This doesn't alter the fact that Borghese was putting together a comic Brancaleone army, where alongside diehard Fascist granddads (Borghese himself was over sixty) were representatives of the state and even divisions of the Forestry Rangers—don't ask why the Forestry Rangers, perhaps with all the deforestation that had gone on after the war, they had nothing better to do. But this motley crew was capable of some nasty things. From later judicial proceedings it emerges that Licio Gelli's role was to capture the president of the republic, at that time Giuseppe Saragat. A ship owner from Civitavecchia had offered the use of his merchant ships to transport those captured by the conspirators to the Lipari Islands. You won't believe who else was involved in the operation. Otto Skorzeny, the man who had freed Mussolini from his brief imprisonment on the Gran Sasso mountain in 1943! He was still around, someone else who had survived the bloody postwar purges unscathed, with links to the CIA. He could ensure that the United States would not oppose the coup so long as a 'moderate democratic' military regime took power. Just think of the hypocrisy there. But what the later investigations never brought to light was that Skorzeny had evidently remained in contact with Mussolini, who owed him a lot—perhaps he would take care of the Duce's return from exile to provide the heroic vision the conspirators needed. In short, the coup depended entirely on Mussolini's triumphal return.

"Just listen to this. The coup had been carefully planned

since 1969, the year of the bombing in Piazza Fontana, which was arranged so all suspicion would fall on the Left and to psychologically prepare public opinion for a return to law and order. Borghese planned to occupy the Ministry of the Interior, the Ministry of Defense, the state television studios, and the communication networks (radio and telephone), and to deport all parliamentary opponents. This isn't some fantasy on my part: a proclamation was later found that Borghese was going to read out on the radio, and which said more or less that the long-awaited time for political change had arrived, that the clique that had governed for twenty-five years had brought Italy to the brink of economic and moral disaster, and that the army and police supported the takeover of political power. Borghese would have ended by saying, 'Italians, in delivering the glorious tricolor back into your hands, we urge you to cry out proudly our hymn of love, *Viva l'Italia*.' Language typical of Mussolini."

On December 7 and 8, 1970, Braggadocio reminded me, several hundred conspirators assembled in Rome, arms and ammunition were distributed, two generals had taken up position at the Ministry of Defense, a group of armed Forestry Rangers were posted at the state television headquarters, and preparations were made in Milan for the occupation of the Sesto San Giovanni quarter, a traditional Communist stronghold.

"Then, all of a sudden, what happens? While the plan seemed to be proceeding smoothly, and we might say the conspirators had Rome within their grasp, Borghese announced that the operation had been called off. Later it was implied that forces loyal to the state were opposed to the conspiracy, but then why not arrest Borghese the day before, rather than wait for uniformed lumberjacks to make their way to Rome? In any event, the whole business is more or less hushed up, those behind the coup slip discreetly away, Borghese takes refuge in Spain, a few idiots get themselves arrested, all of them 'detained' in private clinics, and some visited by General Miceli in their new quarters and promised protection in exchange for silence. Parliamentary inquiries are hardly mentioned by the press, in fact the public is fed vague news about it only three months later. I'm not interested in what actually happened, what I want to know is why a coup so carefully prepared was called off in a matter of a few hours, transforming an extremely serious business into a farce. Why?"

"You tell me."

"I think I'm the only person to have asked the question and certainly the only one to have worked out the answer, which is as plain as day: that very night, news arrives that Mussolini, who is now in Italy ready to resurface, *has suddenly died*—which, at his age, and having been shuttled around, is hardly improbable. The coup is called off because its charismatic symbol is gone, and this time for real, twenty-five years after his supposed death."

Braggadocio's eyes gleamed, appearing to illuminate the lines of skulls that surrounded us, his hands shook, his lips were covered with whitish saliva. He grasped me by the shoulders: "You understand, Colonna, this is my reconstruction of the facts!"

"But if I remember correctly, there was also a trial—"

"A charade, with Andreotti, the then prime minister, helping to cover it all up, and those who ended in jail were minor players. The point is, everything we heard was false or distorted, and for twenty years we've been living a lie. I've always said: never believe what they tell you . . ."

"And your story ends there . . ."

"Eh, no, this is the beginning of another one, and perhaps I only became interested through what happened next, which was the direct consequence of Mussolini's death. Without the figure of the Duce, Gladio could no longer hope to seize power, and meanwhile the prospect of Soviet invasion seemed increasingly remote, since there was now a gradual move toward détente. But Gladio was not disbanded. On the contrary, it became truly active from then on."

"And how was that?"

"Well, since it's no longer a question of establishing a new power by overthrowing the government, Gladio joins up with all the hidden forces trying to destabilize Italy in an effort to prevent the rise of the Left and to prepare the way for new forms of repression, to be carried out in full accordance with the law. Before the Borghese plot, you realize, don't you, that there were very few bomb attacks like Piazza Fontana? Only then do the Red Brigades get going. And the bombings start in the years immediately following, one after another: 1973, a bomb at the police headquarters in Milan; 1974, a massacre in Piazza della Loggia in Brescia; that same year, a high-explosive bomb goes off on the train from Rome to Munich, with twelve dead and forty-eight injured. But remember, Aldo

Moro, foreign minister at the time and soon to be prime minister, was to have been on board, but had missed the train because some ministry officials had made him get off at the last moment to sign some urgent documents. Ten years later, another bomb on the Naples–Milan express. Not to mention the killing of Moro in 1978, and we still don't know what really happened. As if that weren't enough, in that same year, a month after his election, the new pope, John Paul I, died mysteriously. Heart attack or stroke, they said, but why did the pope's personal effects disappear: his glasses, his slippers, his notes, and the bottle of Effortil he apparently had to take for low blood pressure? Why did these things disappear into thin air? Perhaps because it wasn't credible that someone with hypotension would have a stroke? Why was Cardinal Villot the first important person to enter the room immediately after? It's obvious, you'll say—he was the Vatican secretary of state. But a book by a certain David Yallop exposes a number of facts: the pope is rumored to have been interested in the existence of an ecclesiastical-Masonic cabal that included Cardinal Villot, Monsignor Agostino Casaroli, deputy director of the *Osservatore Romano* newspaper and director of Vatican Radio, and of course the ever-present Monsignor Marcinkus, who ruled the roost at the Istituto per le Opere di Religione, better known as the Vatican Bank, and who was later discovered to have been involved in tax evasion and money laundering, and who covered up other dark dealings by such characters as Roberto Calvi and Michele Sindona—both of whom, surprise surprise, would come to a sticky end over the next few years, one hanged under Blackfriars Bridge in London, the other poisoned in prison. A copy of the weekly magazine *Il Mondo* was found on the pope's desk, open to a report on the operations of the Vatican Bank. Yallop suspects six people of the murder: Villot, Cardinal John Cody of Chicago, Marcinkus, Sindona, Calvi, and once again Licio Gelli, the venerable master of the P2 Masonic lodge. You'll tell me this has nothing to do with Gladio, but by sheer coincidence, many of these characters play some part in the other conspiracies, and the Vatican was involved in rescuing and sheltering Mussolini. Perhaps this was what the pope had discovered, though several years had passed since the death of the real Duce, and he wanted to get rid of the gang that had been preparing to overthrow the state since the end of the Second World War. And I should add that with Pope John Paul I dead, the business must have ended up in the hands of John Paul II, shot three years later by the Turkish Grey Wolves, the same Grey Wolves, as I've said, who were a part of the Turkish stay-behind . . . The pope then grants a pardon, his contrite attacker repents in prison, but all in all, the pontiff is frightened off and no longer gets involved in that business, not least because he has no overwhelming interest in Italy and seems preoccupied with fighting Protestant sects in the Third World. And so they leave him be. Aren't all these coincidences proof enough?"

"Or perhaps it's just your tendency to see conspiracies everywhere, so you put two and two together to make five."

"Me? Look at the court cases, it is all there, provided you're able to find your way around the archives. The trouble is, facts get lost between one piece of news and another. Take the story about Peteano. In May 1972, near Gorizia, the police are informed that a Fiat Five Hundred with two bullet holes in the windshield has been abandoned on a certain road. Three policemen arrive; they try to open the hood and are blown up. For some time it's thought to be the work of the Red Brigades, but years later someone by the name of Vincenzo Vinciguerra appears on the scene. And listen to this: after his involvement in other mysterious affairs, he manages to avoid arrest and escapes to Spain, where he is sheltered by the international anticommunist network Aginter Press. Here he makes contact with another right-wing terrorist, Stefano Delle Chiaie, joins the Avanguardia Nazionale, then disappears to Chile and Argentina, but in 1978 he decides, magnanimously, that all this struggle against the state made no sense and he gives himself up in Italy. Note that he didn't repent, he still thought he'd been right to do what he had done up until then, and so, I ask you, why did he give himself up? I'd say out of a need for publicity. There are murderers who return to the scene of the crime, serial killers who send evidence to the police because they want to be caught, otherwise they will not end up on the front page, and so Vinciguerra starts spewing out confession after confession. He accepts responsibility for the explosion at Peteano and points his finger at the security forces who had protected him. Only in 1984 does an investigating judge, Felice Casson, discover that the explosive used at Peteano came from a Gladio arms depot, and most intriguing of all, the existence of that depot was revealed to him—I'll give you a thousand guesses—by Andreotti, who therefore knew and had kept his mouth shut. A police expert (who also happened to be a member of the far-right Ordine Nuovo) had reported that the explosive was identical to that used by the Red Brigades, but Casson established that the explosive was C-4 supplied to NATO forces. In short, a fine web of intrigue, but as you can see, regardless of whether it was NATO or the Red Brigades, Gladio was implicated. Except that the investigations also show that Ordine Nuovo had been working with the Italian military secret service. And you understand that if a military secret service has three policemen blown up, it won't be out of any dislike for the police but to direct the blame at far-left extremists. To make a long story short, after investigations and counterinvestigations, Vinciguerra is sentenced to life in prison, from where he continues to make revelations over the strategy of tension they were conducting. He talks about the bombing of the Bologna railway station (you see how there are links between one bombing and another, it's not just my imagination), and he says that the massacre at Piazza Fontana in 1969 had been planned to force the then prime minister, Mariano Rumor, to declare a state of emergency. He also adds, and I'll read it to you: 'You can't go into hiding without money. You can't go into hiding without support. I could choose the path that others followed, of finding support elsewhere, perhaps in Argentina through the secret services. I could also choose the path of crime. But I have no wish to work with the secret services nor to play the criminal. So to regain my freedom I had only one choice. To give myself up. And this is what I've done.' Obviously it's the logic of an exhibitionist lunatic, but a lunatic who has reliable information. And so this is my story, reconstructed almost in its entirety: the shadow of Mussolini, who is taken for dead, wholly dominates Italian events from 1945 until, I'd say, now. And his real death unleashes the most terrible period in this country's history, involving stay-behind, the CIA, NATO, Gladio, the P2, the Mafia, the secret services, the military top command, prime ministers such as Andreotti and presidents like Cossiga, and naturally a good part of the far-left terrorist organizations, duly infiltrated and manipulated. Not to mention that Moro was kidnapped and assassinated because he knew something and would have talked. And if you want to, you can add lesser criminal cases that have no apparent political relevance . . ."

"Yes, the Beast of Via San Gregorio, the Soap Maker of Correggio, the Monster of the Via Salaria . . ."

"Ah, well, don't be sarcastic. Perhaps not the cases immediately after the war, but for the rest it's more convenient, as they say, to see just one story dominated by a single virtual figure who seemed to direct the traffic from the balcony of Palazzo Venezia, even though no one could see him. Skeletons can always appear at night," he said, pointing to the silent hosts around us, "and perform their *danse macabre*. You know, there are more things in heaven and earth, etc. etc. But it's clear, once the Soviet threat was over, that Gladio was officially consigned to the attic, and both Cossiga and Andreotti talked about it to exorcise its ghost, to present it as something normal that happened with the approval of the authorities, of a community made up of patriots, like the Carbonari in bygone times. But is it really all over, or are certain diehard groups still working away in the shadows? I think there is more to come."

He looked around, frowned: "But we'd better leave now, I don't like the look of that Japanese group coming in. Oriental spies are everywhere, and now that China's at it, they can understand all languages."

As we left, I took a deep breath and asked him, "But you've checked it all out?"

"I've spoken to well-informed people and I've sought the advice of our colleague Lucidi. Perhaps you don't know he has links with the secret services."

"I know, I know. But do you trust him?"

"They're people used to keeping their silence, don't worry. I need a few more days to gather other cast-iron evidence—cast-iron, I say—then I'll go to Simei and present him with the results of my investigation. Twelve installments for twelve zero issues."

That evening, to forget about the bones at San Bernardino, I took Maia out for a candlelight dinner. I didn't of course mention Gladio, I avoided dishes that involved taking anything off the bone, and was slowly emerging from my afternoon ordeal.

16

Saturday, June 6

Braggadocio spent several days that week putting together his scoop and the whole of Thursday morning hunkered down with Simei in his office. They reemerged around eleven o'clock, with Simei commending him, "Check the information once again, thoroughly. I don't want any risks."

"Don't worry," replied Braggadocio, radiating high spirits and optimism. "This evening I'm meeting someone I can trust. I'll do one last check."

Meanwhile the news team were all busily arranging the regular pages for the first zero issue: sports, Palatino's games, letters of denial, horoscopes, and death notices.

"No matter how much we invent," said Costanza at one point, "I'll bet you we won't manage to fill even those twenty-four pages. We need more news."

"All right," said Simei. "Perhaps you can lend a hand, Colonna."

"News doesn't need to be invented," I said. "All you have to do is recycle it."

"How?"

"People have short memories. Taking an absurd example, everyone should know that Julius Caesar was assassinated on the ides of March, but memories get muddled. Take a biography recently published in Britain that reexamines the whole story, and all you have to do is come up with a sensational headline, such as 'Spectacular Discovery by Cambridge Historians: Julius Caesar really assassinated on Ides of March,' you retell the whole story, and turn it into a thoroughly enjoyable article. Now, the Caesar story is something of an exaggeration, I grant you, but if you talk about the Pio Albergo Trivulzio affair, here you can produce an article along the lines of the Banca Romana collapse. That happened at the end of the nineteenth century and has nothing to do with the present scandals, but one scandal leads to another, all you have to do is refer to rumors, and you've got the story of the Banca Romana business as if it happened yesterday. I bet Lucidi would know how to pull a good article out of it."

"Excellent," said Simei. "What is it, Cambria?"

"I see an agency report here, another statue of the Madonna crying in a village down south."

"Terrific, you can turn that into a sensational story!"

"Superstitions all over again—"

"No! We're not a newsletter for the atheistic and rationalist crowd. People want miracles, not trendy skepticism. Writing about a miracle doesn't mean compromising ourselves by saying the newspaper believes it. We recount what's happened, or say that someone has witnessed it. Whether these Virgins actually cry is none of our business. Readers must draw their own conclusions, and if they're believers, they'll believe it. With a headline over several columns."

Everyone worked away in great excitement. I passed Maia's desk, where she was concentrating on the death notices, and said, "And don't forget, 'Family bereft—'"

"'—and good friend Filiberto shares the grief of beloved Matilde and dearest children Mario and Serena,'" she replied.

"You have to keep up with the times—the new Italian names are Jessyka with a *y* or Samanta without the *h,* and even Sue Ellen, written 'Sciuellen.'" I gave her a smile of encouragement and moved on.

I spent the evening at Maia's place, succeeding, as happened now and then, in making a cozy love nest out of that bleak den piled with precarious towers of books.

Among the piles were many classical records, vinyl inherited from her grandparents. Sometimes we lay there for hours listening. That evening Maia put on Beethoven's Seventh, and she told me, her eyes brimming with tears, how ever since her adolescence, the second movement would make her cry. "It started when I was sixteen. I had no money, and thanks to someone I knew, I managed to slip into a concert without paying, except that I had no seat, so I squatted down on the steps in the upper balcony, and little by little I found myself almost lying down. The wood was hard, but I didn't feel a thing. And during the second movement I thought that's how I'd like to die, and burst into tears. I was crazy then, but I went on crying even after I'd grown up."

I had never cried listening to music, but was moved by the fact that she did. After several minutes' silence, Maia said, "He was a fruitcake." He who? But Schumann, of course, said Maia, as if I had become distracted. Her autism, as usual.

"Schumann a fruitcake?"

"Yes, loads of romantic outpouring, what you'd expect for that period, but all too cerebral. And by straining his brain he went mad. I can see why his wife fell in love with Brahms. Another temperament, other music, and a bon vivant. Mind you, I'm not saying Robert was bad, I'm sure he had talent, he wasn't one of those blusterers."

"Which?"

"Like that bumptious Liszt, or the rambunctious Rachmaninoff. They wrote some terrible music, all stuff for effect, for making money, Concerto for Goons in C Major, things like that. If you look, you'll find none of their records in that pile. I dumped them. They'd have been better off as farm hands."

"But who do you think is better than Liszt?"

"Satie, no?"

"But you don't cry over Satie, do you?"

"Of course not, he wouldn't have wanted it, I only cry over the second movement of the Seventh." Then, after a moment's pause, "I also cry over some Chopin, since my adolescence. Not his concertos, of course."

"Why not his concertos?"

"Because if you took him away from the piano and put him in front of an orchestra, he would have no idea where he was. He wrote piano parts for strings, brass, even drums. And then, have you seen that film with Cornel Wilde playing Chopin and splashing a drop of blood on the keyboard? What would have happened if he'd conducted an orchestra? He'd have splashed blood on the first violin."

Maia never ceased to amaze me, even when I thought I knew her well. With her, I would have learned to appreciate music. Her way, in any case.

It was our last evening of happiness. Yesterday I woke late and didn't get to the office until late morning. As I entered, I could see men in uniform searching through Braggadocio's drawers and a plainclothesman questioning those present. Simei stood sallow-faced at the door of his office.

Cambria approached, speaking softly, as if he had some secret to tell: "They've killed Braggadocio."

"What? Braggadocio? How?"

"A night watchman was returning home on his bike this morning at six and saw a body lying face-down, wounded in the back. At that hour it took him some time to find a bar that was open so he could telephone for an ambulance and the police. One stab wound, that's what the police doctor found right away, just one, but inflicted with force. No sign of the knife."

"Where?"

"In an alleyway around Via Torino, what's it called . . . Via Bagnara, or Bagnera."

The plainclothesman introduced himself. He was a police inspector and asked when I had last seen Braggadocio. "Here in the office, yesterday," I replied, "like all my colleagues, I suspect. Then I think he went off alone, just before the others."

He asked how I had spent my evening, as I imagine he'd done with the rest. I said I'd had supper with a friend and then gone straight to bed. Clearly I didn't have an alibi, but it seems none of those present had one either, and the inspector didn't seem overly concerned. It was just a routine question, as they say on TV cop shows.

He was more interested in whether Braggadocio had any enemies, whether he was pursuing dangerous inquiries. I was hardly about to tell him everything, not because there was anyone I was anxious to protect, but I was beginning to realize that if someone had bumped off Braggadocio, it had to do with his investigations. And I had the sudden feeling that if I'd shown even the smallest sign of knowing anything, I too might be worth getting rid of. I mustn't tell the police, I thought. Hadn't Braggadocio told me that everyone was implicated in his stories, including the Forestry Rangers? And though I'd regarded him as a crank until yesterday, his death now assured him a certain credibility.

I was sweating. The inspector didn't seem to notice, or perhaps he put it down to momentary distress.

"I'm not sure what Braggadocio was up to these past few days," I said. "Maybe Dottor Simei can tell you, he assigns the articles. I think he was working on something to do with prostitution. I don't know if that's of any help."

"We shall see," said the inspector, and he moved on to question Maia, who was crying. She had no love for Braggadocio, I thought, but murder is murder. Poor dear. I felt sorry not for Braggadocio but for Maia—she'd probably be feeling guilty for speaking ill of him.

At that moment Simei motioned me to his office. "Colonna," he said, sitting down at his desk, his hands trembling, "you know what Braggadocio was working on."

"I do and I don't. He mentioned something, but I'm not sure that—"

"Colonna, don't beat around the bush, you know perfectly well that Braggadocio was stabbed because he was about to reveal important information. Now I don't know what was true and what he invented, though it's clear that if his inquiry covered a hundred stories, he must have gotten to the truth on at least one of them, and that is why he was silenced. But since he told me all of it yesterday, it means I also know that one story, though I don't know which it is. And since he told me that he told you, you know it too. So we're both in danger. To make matters worse, two hours ago I got a call from Commendator Vimercate. He didn't say who told him, or what he'd been told, but Vimercate found out that the entire *Domani* venture was too dangerous even for him, so he decided to shut the whole thing down. He's sent me checks for journalists—they'll each get an envelope with two months' salary and a few words of thanks. None of them had a contract, so they can't complain. Vimercate didn't know you were in danger as well, but I think you might find it difficult to go around banking a check, so I'm tearing it up—I have some money in hand, your pay packet will contain two months' in cash. The offices will be dismantled by tomorrow evening. As for us two, you can forget our agreement, your little job, the book you were going to write. *Domani* is being axed, right now. Even with the newspaper shut, you and I know too much."

"I think Braggadocio told Lucidi as well."

"You haven't understood a thing, have you. That was where he went wrong. Lucidi sniffed out that our dear departed friend was handling something dangerous and went straight off to report it. To whom? I don't know, but certainly to someone who decided that Braggadocio knew too much. No one's going to hurt Lucidi, he's on the other side of the barricade, but they might harm us. I'll tell you what I'm going to do. As soon as the police are out of here, I'm putting the rest of the cash in my bag, shooting straight down to the station, and taking the first train for Switzerland. With no luggage. I know someone there who can change a person's identity, new name, new passport, new residence—we'll have to work out where. I'm disappearing before Braggadocio's killers can find me. I hope I'll beat them to it. And I've asked Vimercate to pay me in dollars on Credit Suisse. As for you, I don't know what to suggest, but first of all, don't go wandering the streets, lock yourself up at home. Then find a way of disappearing, I'd choose eastern Europe, where stay-behind didn't exist."

"But you think it's all to do with stay-behind? That's already in the public domain. Or perhaps the business about Mussolini? That's so outlandish no one would believe it."

"And the Vatican? Even if the story wasn't true, it would

still end up in the papers that the Church had covered up Mussolini's escape in 1945 and had sheltered him for nearly fifty years. With all the troubles they already have down there with Sindona, Calvi, Marcinkus, and the rest, before they've managed to prove the Mussolini business a hoax, the scandal would be all over the international press. Trust no one, Colonna, lock yourself up at home, tonight at least, then think about getting away. You've enough to live on for a few months. And if you go, let's say, to Romania, it costs nothing there, and with the twelve million lire in this envelope you could live like a lord for some time. After that, well, you can see. Goodbye, Colonna, I'm sorry things have ended this way. It's like that joke our Maia told about the cowboy at Abilene: Too bad, we've lost. If you'll excuse me, I'd better get ready to leave as soon as the police have gone."

I wanted to get out of there right away, but that damned inspector went on questioning us, getting nowhere fast. Meanwhile evening fell.

I walked past Lucidi's desk as he was opening his envelope. "Have you received your just reward?" I asked, and he clearly understood what I was referring to.

He looked me up and down and asked, "What did Braggadocio tell you?"

"I know he was following some line of inquiry, but he wouldn't tell me exactly what."

"Really?" he said. "Poor devil, who knows what he's been up to." And then he turned away.

Once the inspector had said I could leave, with the usual warning to remain available for further questioning, I whispered to Maia, "Go home. Wait there until I phone you, probably not before tomorrow morning."

She looked at me, terrified. "But how are you involved in all this?"

"I'm not, I'm not, what are you thinking, I'm just upset."

"Tell me what's going on. They've given me an envelope with a check and many thanks for my invaluable services."

"They're closing the newspaper. I'll explain later."

"Why not tell me now?"

"Tomorrow, I swear I'll tell you everything. You stay safe at home. Just do as I say, please."

She listened, her eyes welling with tears. And I left without saying another word.

I spent the evening at home, eating nothing, draining half a bottle of whiskey, and thinking what to do next. I felt exhausted, took a sleeping pill, and fell asleep.

And this morning, no water in the tap.

17

Saturday, June 6, Noon

There. Now I've told it all. Let me try to make sense of it. Who are "they"? That's what Simei said, that Braggadocio had pieced together a number of facts, correctly or incorrectly. Which of these facts could worry somebody? The business about Mussolini? And in that case, who had the guilty conscience? The Vatican? Or perhaps conspirators in the Borghese plot who still held authority (though after twenty years they all must be dead), or the secret services (which?). Or perhaps not. Perhaps it was just some old Fascist who's haunted by the past and acted alone, perhaps getting pleasure from threatening Vimercate, as though he had—who knows?—the Sacra Corona Unita behind him. A nutcase, then, but if a nutcase is trying to do away with you, he's just as dangerous as someone who's sane, and more so. For example, whether it's "they" or some lone nutcase, someone entered my house last night. And having gotten in once, they or he could get in a second time. So I'd better not stay here. But then, is this nutcase or are these "they" so sure I know something? Did Braggadocio say anything about me to Lucidi? Maybe not, or not much, judging from my last exchange of remarks with that sneak. But can I feel safe? Certainly not. It's a long step, though, between that and escaping to Romania—best to see what happens, read the newspapers tomorrow. If they don't mention the killing of Braggadocio, things are worse than I imagine—it means someone's trying to hush it all up. I've got to hide at least for a while. But where? Right now it would be dangerous to stick my nose outside.

I thought about Maia and her hideaway at Orta. My affair with Maia has passed, I think, unnoticed, and she shouldn't be under surveillance. She no, but my telephone yes, so I can't telephone her from home, and to telephone from outside means I have to go out.

It occurred to me that there was a back entrance, from the courtyard below, through the toilets, to the local bar. I also remembered a metal gate at the far end of the courtyard that had been locked for decades. My landlord had told me about it when he handed me the keys to the apartment. Along with the key to the main entrance and the landing door, there was another one, old and rusty. "You'll never need it," said the landlord with a smile, "but every tenant has had one for the past fifty years. We had no air-raid shelter here during the war, you see, and there was a fairly large one in the house behind, on Via Quarto dei Mille, the road that runs parallel to ours. So a passageway was opened up at the far end of the courtyard for families to reach the shelter quickly if the alarm sounded. The gate has remained locked from both sides, but each of our tenants had a key, and as you see, in almost fifty years it's become rusty. I don't suppose you'll ever need it, but that gate is also a good escape route in the event of fire. You can put the key in a drawer, if you wish, and forget about it."

That's what I had to do. I went downstairs and into the bar through the back door. The manager knows me, and I've done it before. I looked around. Hardly anyone there in the morning. Just an elderly couple sitting at a table with two cappuccinos and two croissants, and they didn't look like secret agents. I ordered a double coffee—I still wasn't properly awake—and went to the telephone booth. Maia answered immediately in great agitation, and I told her to keep calm and listen.

"So follow carefully, and no questions. Pack a bag with enough for a few days at Orta, then get your car. Behind where I live, in Via Quarto dei Mille, I'm not sure what number, there'll be an entranceway, more or less the same distance up the road as my place. It could be open, because I think it goes into a courtyard where there's a workshop of some kind. Either go in, or you can wait outside. Synchronize your watch with mine, you should be able to get there in fifteen minutes, let's say we'll meet in exactly an hour. If the entrance gate is closed, I'll be waiting for you outside, but get there on time, I don't want to hang around in the street. Please, don't ask any questions. Take your bag, get in the car, make sure you have the timing right, and come. Then I'll tell you everything. Check the rearview mirror every now and then, and if you think someone's tailing you, use your imagination, do some crazy turns to throw them off. It's not so easy along the canals, but after that, lots of ways to give them the slip, jump the lights on red. I trust you, my love."

Maia could have had a promising career in armed robbery. She did things to perfection, and within the agreed hour, there she was in the entranceway, tense but happy.

I jumped into the car, told her where to turn to reach Viale Certosa as quickly as possible, and from there she knew her way to the highway for Novara, and then the turnoff for Orta, better than I did.

We hardly spoke during the entire trip. Once we'd reached the house, I told her it might be risky for her to know all that I knew. Would she prefer to rely on me and remain in the dark? But I should have guessed, there was no question. "Excuse me," she said, "I still don't know who or what you're frightened of, but either no one knows we're together, in which case I'm in no danger, or they'll find out and be convinced I know. So spit it out, otherwise how will I ever think what you think?"

Undaunted. I had to tell her everything—after all, she was now flesh of my flesh, as the Good Book says.

18

Thursday, June 11

For several days I barricaded myself in the house, afraid to go out. "Come on," said Maia, "no one in this place knows you, and those you're scared of, whoever they are, have no idea you're here."

"It doesn't matter," I replied, "you can never be too sure."

Maia began treating me like an invalid. She gave me tranquilizers, stroked the back of my neck as I sat at the window gazing out at the lake.

On Sunday morning she went off early to buy the papers. The killing of Braggadocio was reported on an inside page, without much prominence: journalist murdered, may have been investigating a prostitution ring, attacked by pimp.

It seemed the police had accepted the idea, following what I had said, and perhaps after hints from Simei. They were clearly not thinking about us journalists, nor did they appear to have noticed that Simei and I had gone missing. If they'd returned to the office, they would have found it empty, and besides, the inspector hadn't bothered to take down our addresses. A fine Maigret he'd have been. But I don't imagine he's worrying about us. Prostitution was the more convenient lead, routine stuff. Costanza could have told him, of course, that it was he who was investigating those women, but he may also have thought Braggadocio's death had something to do with that story, and he might have begun to fear for his life and kept quiet as a mouse.

Next day Braggadocio had even vanished from the inside pages. The police must have had plenty of cases like his and, after all, the dead man was no more than a fourth-rate hack. Round up the usual suspects, and be done with it.

At dusk I watched as the lake darkened. The island of San Giulio, so radiant under the sun, rose from the water like Böcklin's *Isle of the Dead.*

Maia decided to try to put me back on my feet, so she took me for a walk on the Sacro Monte. I'd never been there before. It's a series of chapels on the top of a hill with mystical dioramas of polychrome statues in natural settings, smiling angels but above all scenes from the life of Saint Francis. In the scene of a mother hugging a suffering child, I saw, alas, the victims of some remote terrorist attack. In a solemn meeting with a pope, various cardinals, and somber Capuchin friars, I saw a council meeting at the Vatican Bank planning my capture. Nor were all those colors and other pious terracottas enough to make me think of the Kingdom of Heaven: everything seemed a perfidiously disguised allegory of infernal forces plotting in the shadows. I went as far as imagining that those figures at night would become skeletons (what, after all, is the pink body of an angel if not a deceptive integument that cloaks a skeleton, even if it's a celestial one?) and join in the *danse macabre* in the Church of San Bernardino alle Ossa.

Indeed, I never believed I could have been quite so faint-hearted, and felt ashamed to let Maia see me in such a state (there, I thought, she too is going to ditch me), but the image of Braggadocio lying face-down in Via Bagnera remained before my eyes.

From time to time I hoped it might have been Boggia, the killer from a hundred years ago, who had materialized at night in Via Bagnera, through a sudden rent in time and space (what did Vonnegut call it? a chrono-synclastic infundibulum), and disposed of the intruder. But this didn't explain the telephone call to Vimercate, the point I used with Maia when she suggested that perhaps it was a two-bit crime, that you could see right away that Braggadocio was a dirty old man, God rest his soul, that perhaps he'd been trying to take advantage of one of those women, hence the vendetta by the pimp looking after her, a simple matter, where *de minimis non curat praetor*—the law doesn't concern itself with trifles. "Yes," I repeated, "but a pimp doesn't telephone a publisher to get him to close down a newspaper!"

"But who says Vimercate actually received the call? Maybe he'd changed his mind about the whole enterprise, it was costing him too much. And as soon as he found out about the death of one of his reporters, he used it as a pretext to close down *Domani*, paying two months' instead of a year's salary. Or maybe . . . you told me he wanted *Domani* so that someone would say, Put an end to it and I'll let you into the inner sanctum. Well then, suppose that someone like Lucidi passed on news to the inner sanctum that *Domani* was about to publish an embarrassing series of articles. They telephone Vimercate and say, All right, give up this gutter rag and we'll let you into the club. Then, quite independently, Braggadocio gets killed, perhaps by the usual nutcase, and you've eliminated the problem of the telephone call to Vimercate."

"But I haven't eliminated the nutcase. Who crept into my house at night?"

"You've told me that story. How can you be sure someone came in?"

"So who turned off the water?"

"But listen to me. You have a woman who comes in to clean?"

"Only once a week."

"When was she last there?"

"She always comes Friday afternoons. And, as it happens, that was the day we found out about Braggadocio."

"So? Couldn't she have turned off the water because of the drip from the shower?"

"But on that Friday evening I had a glass of water to swallow down a sleeping pill . . ."

"You'd have had half a glass, that was all you needed. Even with the water turned off there's always some in the pipe, and you simply hadn't noticed. Did you drink any more water that evening?"

"No, I didn't even have supper, I just finished off half a bottle of whiskey."

"You see? I'm not saying you're paranoid, but with Braggadocio killed and what Simei had told you, you jumped to the conclusion that someone had broken into your house that night. In fact, no, it was the cleaning lady, that afternoon."

"They made short work of killing Braggadocio!"

"That's another matter. So it's quite possible no one's interested in you."

We have spent the past four days pondering, constructing, and ruling out possibilities, I getting gloomier, Maia ever more obliging, moving untiringly back and forth between house and town to buy fresh food and bottles of malt whiskey, of which I have drained three. We made love twice, though I did it with anger, as if to get something out of my system, with no feeling of pleasure. Even so, I felt more in love with that creature who, from a sheltered sparrow, had transformed into a faithful she-wolf, ready to bite whoever might want to harm me.

That was until this evening, when we switched on the TV and found ourselves, almost by chance, watching a program about a British documentary called *Operation Gladio,* just broadcast by the BBC.

We watched in amazement, speechless.

It seemed like a film by Braggadocio. It included everything that Braggadocio had imagined and then some, but the words were backed up by photographs and other documentation, and were those of well-known personalities. It began with the activities of the Belgian stay-behind and confirmed, yes, that the existence of Gladio had been revealed to heads of government, but only to those the CIA trusted, so Moro and Fanfani were kept in the dark. Appearing over the screen were declarations by leading spies, such as, "Deception is a state of mind, and the mind of the state." Vincenzo Vinciguerra appeared throughout the two-and-a-half-hour program, revealing all. He even said that before the end of the war the Allied secret services had gotten Borghese and his men of the Decima Mas commando unit to sign an undertaking for future collaboration in opposing a Soviet invasion, and the various witnesses confirmed openly that for an operation like Gladio it was only natural that the enlisted had to be ex-Fascists—in Germany the American secret services had even guaranteed immunity to a butcher like Klaus Barbie.

Licio Gelli appeared several times, declaring that he had collaborated with the Allied secret services, though Vinciguerra described him as a good Fascist, and Gelli spoke about his exploits, his contacts, his sources of information, not worrying about what was patently obvious—that he had always played a double game.

Cossiga told how in 1948, as a young Catholic militant, he had been provided with a Sten gun and grenades, ready to go into action if the Communist Party had not accepted the election results. Vinciguerra calmly restated how the whole of the Far Right was devoted to a strategy of increasing tension to psychologically prepare the public for a state of emergency, but he emphasized that Ordine Nuovo and Avanguardia Nazionale were working together with senior officials from the various ministries. Senators at the parliamentary inquiry stated in no uncertain terms that the secret services and police had fiddled with the paperwork for each bomb attack to paralyze the judicial investigations. Vinciguerra explained that those responsible for the bomb attack at Piazza Fontana were not just Franco Freda and Giovanni

Ventura, whom everyone considered to be the masterminds; the entire operation had been directed by the Special Affairs Office of the Ministry of the Interior. Then the program looked at the ways in which Ordine Nuovo and Avanguardia Nazionale had infiltrated left-wing groups to incite them to commit acts of terrorism. Colonel Oswald Lee Winter, a CIA man, stated that the Red Brigades had not only been infiltrated, but took their orders from General Santovito, head of the Italian Military Intelligence and Security Service.

In a mind-boggling interview, one of the founders of the Red Brigades, Alberto Franceschini, among the very first to have been arrested, was appalled at the thought that, acting in good faith, he had been spurred on by someone else for other motives. And Vinciguerra stated that Avanguardia Nazionale had been given the task of distributing Maoist manifestoes to increase fear about pro-Chinese activities.

One of the commanders of Gladio, General Inzerilli, had no hesitation in saying that arms deposits were kept at police stations and that members of Gladio could help themselves by showing half of a one-thousand-lire note as a sign of recognition, like in a cheap spy story. It ended, of course, with the killing of Aldo Moro, and secret service agents were spotted in Via Fani at the time of the kidnapping, one of them claiming he was in that area for lunch with a friend, though it was nine in the morning.

William Colby, the former head of the CIA, denied everything, but other CIA agents, appearing full face, spoke of documents that gave details about payments made by the organization to people involved in terrorist attacks—five thousand dollars a month, for example, to General Miceli.

As the television documentary outlined, all was hearsay, on the basis of which no one could be convicted, but it was quite enough to trouble public opinion.

Maia and I were bewildered. The revelations went far beyond Braggadocio's wildest fantasies. "Of course," said Maia, "he himself told you that all this news had been circulating for some time, it had just been wiped from the collective memory. All that needed to be done was go through the newspaper archives and put the pieces of the mosaic back together. I too read the newspapers, not just when I was a student but when I was working on celebrity romance stories, and, as you might guess, I discussed these things, except that I would also forget them, as if one new revelation canceled out the other. All you have to do is bring it out. Braggadocio did it, and the BBC has done it."

"Yes, but Braggadocio probably added something of his own, like the story about Mussolini, or the killing of John Paul I."

"All right, he was a crank, he saw conspiracies everywhere, but the problem remains the same."

"God in heaven!" I said. "A few days ago someone killed Braggadocio for fear that this news would get out, and now, with the documentary, millions of people will know about it!"

"My love," said Maia, "lucky for you! Let's assume there really was someone, whether the phantom 'they' or the reclusive nutcase, afraid that people might once again remember those events, or that some minor detail might reemerge that perhaps even we who watched the program had failed to notice, something that might still cause trouble for some group or individual . . . Well, after this program, neither 'they' nor the nutcase have any reason whatever for getting rid of you or Simei. If you two decided tomorrow to go and tip off the newspapers about what Braggadocio had confided in you, they'd look at you as if you were two cranks, repeating what you've seen on TV."

"But perhaps someone fears we might talk about what the BBC didn't say, about Mussolini, about John Paul I."

"Fine. Imagine telling them the story about Mussolini. It was fairly improbable when Braggadocio spun it, no proof, just off-the-wall conjectures. They'd say you were overexcited, carried away by the BBC program, let your personal fantasies run wild. In fact, you'd be playing their game. See, they'll say, from now on every schemer is going to come up with something new. And the spreading of these revelations will lead to the suspicion that even those told by the BBC were the result of journalistic speculation, or of delirium, like the conspiracy theories that the Americans didn't really go to the Moon or that the Pentagon is trying to hush up the existence of UFOs. This television program makes all other revelations entirely pointless and ridiculous, because, as you know, *la réalité dépasse la fiction,* and so, now, no one's able to invent anything."

"So I'm free?"

"Who was it said the truth shall set you free? This truth will make every other revelation seem like a lie. In the end, the BBC has done a great service. As of tomorrow, you can go around saying that the pope slits the throats of babies and eats them, or that Mother Teresa of Calcutta was the one who put the bomb on the Munich train, and people will say, 'Oh, really? Interesting,' and they'll turn around and get on with what they were doing. I'll bet you anything that tomorrow's newspapers won't even mention this program. Nothing can upset us any longer in this country. We've seen the barbarian invasions, the sack of Rome, the slaughter of Senigallia, six hundred thousand killed in the Great War and the inferno of the Second, so no one's going to care about a few hundred people it's taken forty years to blow up. Corruption in the secret services? That's a joke compared with the Borgia family. We've always been a people of daggers and poison. We're immune: whenever they tell us some new story or other, we say we've heard worse, and claim it's false. If the United States, half of Europe's secret services, and our government and the newspapers have all lied, why shouldn't the BBC have also lied? The only serious concern for decent citizens is how to avoid paying taxes, and those in charge can do what they like—they always have their snouts in the same trough. Amen. See, two months with Simei and I've become just as sly as everyone else."

"So what are we going to do?"

"First, calm down. Tomorrow I'll go to the bank and quietly cash Vimercate's check, and you can draw out whatever you have, if you've got any."

"I've been saving since April, so I also have two months' salary, around ten million lire, plus the twelve that Simei gave me the other day. I'm rich."

"Wonderful. I've also put something aside. We'll take the lot and run."

"Run? Aren't we now saying we can wander around with nothing to fear?"

"Yes, but do you really want to live in this country, where everything will continue as it always has, where you go to a pizzeria and worry whether the person at the next table might be a secret agent, or might be about to murder another magistrate, setting off the bomb as you're walking past?"

"But where do we go? You've seen, heard how the same things were happening throughout Europe, from Sweden to Portugal. Do you want to end up in Turkey among the Grey Wolves, or in America, if they let you in, where they kill presidents and where maybe the Mafia has infiltrated the CIA? The world's a nightmare, my love. I'd like to get off, but they tell me we can't, we're on an express train."

"Darling, we'll look for a country with no secrets and where everything is done in the open. In Central and South America you'll find plenty. Nothing's hidden, you know who belongs to which drug cartel, who runs the bands of revolutionaries. You sit in a restaurant, a group of friends passes and introduces you to the man in charge of arms smuggling, all neatly shaved and perfumed, dressed in a starched white shirt that hangs loose from his trousers, the waiters address him reverently with *señor* here and *señor* there, and the chief of the Guardia Civil goes across to pay his respects. They are countries that hold no mysteries, everything is done in the open, the police demand to be bribed as a matter of right, the government and the underworld coexist by constitutional decree, the banks make their living through money laundering, and you'll be in trouble if you don't have other money of doubtful provenance, they'll cancel your residency permit. And they kill, but only each other, they leave tourists in peace. We could find work on a newspaper or in a publishing house. I have friends who work down there in the celebrity romance magazines—a good, honest job, now I come to think of it, the articles are trash but everyone knows it, and they find them amusing. And those celebrities whose intimate secrets you're about to reveal have already revealed them the day before on television. It takes only a week to learn Spanish, and then we can find our South Sea island, my Tusitala."

I can never start anything on my own, but if someone passes me the ball, I sometimes manage to score a goal. The fact is that Maia is still quite ingenuous, whereas age has made me wise. And if you know you're a loser, the only consolation is to think that everyone around you, even the winners, are losing out.

That's how I answered Maia.

"You're forgetting, my love, that Italy is slowly turning into one of those havens you want to banish yourself to. If we've managed to both accept and forget all those things the BBC has recounted, it means we are getting used to the idea of losing the sense of shame. Didn't you see that all those interviewed were happily telling us what they'd done and were almost expecting a medal for it? No more Baroque chiaroscuro, everything in broad daylight, as though painted by the impressionists: corruption rife, Mafiosi officially in parliament, tax dodgers in government, and the only ones to end up in prison are Albanian chicken thieves. Decent people will carry on voting for the hoodlums because they won't believe the BBC, or they don't watch such programs because they're glued to trash, perhaps Vimercate's home shopping channels will end up on early evening television, and if someone important is murdered, he gets a state funeral. Let's escape: I'll go back to translating, you go back to your magazines for ladies' hairdressing salons and dentists' waiting rooms. Meanwhile a good film in the evening, weekends here at Orta—and to hell with everyone else. All we have to do is wait: once this country of ours has finally joined the Third World, the living will be easy, as if it were all Copacabana, the hottest spot south of Havana."

Maia has restored my peace of mind, my self-confidence, or at least my calm distrust of the world around me. Life is bearable, you just have to make the most of it. Tomorrow (as Scarlett O'Hara said, another quote, I know, but I've stopped talking myself and have let others take over), tomorrow is another day.

The island of San Giulio will shine again in the sunlight.